Baptized
in Dirty Water

by Joe McQuade

Tafford Publishing

Houston

For Rae, the love of my life

Tafford Publishing
P.O. Box 271804, Houston, Texas 77277

ISBN 0-9623712-8-9
Library of Congress Catalog Card Number 95-62288

Printed in the United States of America
on acid-free paper

Cover Art
© Copyright 1996 by Carla Cheshire

Back Cover Photo
© Copyright 1996 by Louise Dalton

Baptized
in Dirty Water

Prologue

Back in my pink and innocent days, before Donna, before Sharlene, before I even knew what a shrimp boat was, I lived for a time with a quiet guy who knew what it was to fail. The way he told it, and he only told it once, failure was something that left him feeling more lucky than sad.

My friend was sixteen when it happened, the moment that barred him forever from the pantheon of heroes. Sixteen is a tender age for disappointment, but he said it couldn't have come at a better time.

He was wading in a swift river, fishing with a spinning reel while his nine-year-old sister played on the bank. The shores were dark and damp from a recent rain, and the water was so fresh that the fish took little interest in his bait. Eventually he wandered deeper than he should have. The sand gave way, and he found himself rolling in a jumble of fishing line and fast water. His sister was a third his size and barely a swimmer, but she plunged in after him and soon found herself in even worse trouble.

My friend grabbed wildly at a tree root and felt it take hold. The current brought his sister to him, out of control and choking for air. She grabbed his ankle. He felt the extra weight test the root. He kicked her loose. They found her body two days later.

"I'm one of the fortunate few," he told me. "I've had my moment of truth, the chance men rarely have to measure themselves against moral and physical terror."

I remember feeling a prickle of impatience when he said that. Existential despair was already oozing from every crevice of our college dorm.

"You're being too hard on yourself," I said. "There was nothing profound in what you did. It was just a reflex."

He shook his head.

"When she grabbed my foot, time stood still. I could hear the root cracking, my sister choking. I could feel the water sucking us away.

"I knew if I lost that root there was a chance I might drown. I also knew that if my sister had to swim alone, she would surely die. It wasn't a reflex that made me kick. I made a decision."

So he had failed, and he knew it. The choices had been clear—there was no mitigating factor, no room to spin rationalizations. It had been a pure test of virtue and courage that forced his true nature to assert itself. He would begin his life with a dark awareness that others spend a lifetime avoiding. And he said he felt lucky for it.

I asked him what kind of comfort such an insight could possibly provide.

"It's simple," he said. "I am free."

I haven't seen my roommate in years, but I think of him often. Not long after we left the dorm, I came to a predicament he would have considered a test of my virtue and courage. But my case was different, so very different, and I came away from it feeling neither lucky nor free. For years when I thought of Donna, or of Sharlene as last I saw her, nothing was certain or clear. I didn't even know whether I had failed, and in a sense that was the most painful failure of all.

But time, as it does for the fortunate, began to burn away the mist. It was a long and uncertain trip from there to here, but now I understand what became of me under the hot, malevolent stare of the Texas coast. This is the story of my moment of truth, the story of what I did when my hand was on the root.

*   *   *

My guess is that everyone, with the possible exceptions of enthroned royalty and the Baptist clergy, trudges through life with some measure of uncertainty about himself. After all, suspicion of the self is a large part of what it means to be human. Frogs and newts slide through life without a sliver of doubt, but lives there a man with ego so hale that he hasn't chewed a lip and wondered: Am I up to it? Am I worthy? There's a little of the mope in all of us.

What sets me apart from the average mope is the way uncertainty yanks me around on a tight leather choker. That's what got me in trouble in the first place, and the trouble I got into made things even worse.

After Donna, I loitered a lot on what my old roommate might have called my moral worth. It wasn't the easiest way to start the day, but at least it was a change of pace. Before Donna, or for the first half of my life, the hot topic was whether I had the makings of what might be called a man—a tough and courageous fellow who faced adversity with a private smirk. The evidence of my youth was discouraging.

Once when I was a reed-legged whelp of twelve, a friend and I took hold of his little sister to throw her into a swimming pool. My friend swung the girl by her wrists, I by the ankles, while their mother looked on with a tolerant concern. Her husband, a red-faced German, a retired Air Force colonel, a weight bench enthusiast when Schwarzenegger was still pumping his mother's pecs, tapped a giant fist against his chin and studied us.

I was accustomed to starting games with "One, two, three, go." My friend, perhaps acting on a genetic predisposition for the waltz, was in the habit of releasing on the third beat, which he did, leaving me to hold his helpless sister upside down as her head slammed into the side of the pool.

Her father leaped from his chair and sprinted toward me, commanding the attention of everyone at poolside by bellowing his views on goddamn stupid horseplay. Of course, I froze. The girl struggled frantically to get free, but it didn't seem right to just drop her in the water. I squeezed her ankles to my chest and tried to pull up, effectively keeping her face submerged six inches below the surface. To the colonel, it must have appeared I was bent on drowning his daughter before his very eyes.

He took her ankles from me with one hand, pushed me into the pool with the other, and lifted the girl, unharmed but hysterical, into his massive arms. Ten minutes later we were all in the colonel's station wagon, driving home in silence.

All boys suffer humiliations of one kind or another. But for me they were a daily routine, like oatmeal. I could fill volumes on that subject alone, but it would keep me from Donna, and she is what this is about. So, at the outset, let this suffice: My life had pretty much taken the swagger out of me by the time I had to decide what to do with it.

*   *   *

My father, always and everywhere a creature of habit, reacted predictably when I told him my plan for the summer of 1974.

There was a pause, and I knew he was holding the phone before him like the RCA dog beholding its master.

"You sure about this?" I whispered to myself.

"You sure about this?" he said.

Yes, I was sure. No, I appreciated it, but there was nothing he could say to change my mind.

I heard the rasp of his beard against the mouthpiece, and I braced for the worst.

"Well, a man's gotta do what a man's gotta do."

There it was. He couldn't just call me an ungrateful son or tell me I'd broken his widowed father's heart. No, he had to dust off the old haymaker.

"You're right, Dad. He sure does."

I listened. He was behind me one hundred percent. I always had a home to come home to. He knew everything would work out for the best. Good old Dad. His cliches always floated down around me like cool silk scarves—except, of course, for the haymaker.

In my bedroom late at night, I used to hear him tell Mom what a man's gotta do when he can't keep eighteen men on a payroll, or when he has a sweet little bookkeeper who, God bless her, can't count to five. I heard what a man's gotta do when I put a BB through our picture window and asked why a man had to lose his allowance until the bill was paid.

What's a man gotta do? What he's gotta do. The perfect circle, apropos to everything. Coming from men as strong and decent as my father, this refers to the necessity—not the desire, not the attempt, but the necessity—to do the right thing, to live a good life. Oh, did those words sting.

He didn't have to tell me that taking off for the waterfront was ridiculous. I'd grown up in landlocked Fort Worth and didn't know the first thing about shrimping. Fathers don't put their sons and sole heirs through college in hopes they'll cull fish. Worse, there was no way to adorn my flight to Galveston Bay with the slimmest thread of the imperative. I wasn't going because I had to, or because it was the only way a man could be true to his dream. I was going because sometimes a man doesn't know what he's gotta do.

In the terrifying spring of 1974, all this man knew was what he didn't wanna do. Try as I might to accept my father's largesse, I was a sobering flower child who couldn't see himself in the soft seat at a twelve-bay auto body shop. Graduate school would have been a cozy bed, yes, but I had a screaming case of bed sores after four years of Austin pleasure-tripping. Standing on the threshold, clasping my English degree, I was qualified for anything, everything, nothing. The callow face in the bathroom mirror was getting harder and harder to see.

Life! That's it. Experience! Go build yourself a character, young man. Job interviews! Shit.

I wanted to work—needed to—but the mere thought of job hunting made my eyes burn. Asking for a job, competing for a job, succeeding at a job—what a dreary agony it is to begin a career. All my life I had anticipated the wondrous moment when I could put away the books and forge a passage of my own in the world. But suddenly the moment was upon me, and I couldn't find the strength to put one foot in front of the other. In one of my lowest moments that spring, I even condemned myself for not joining ROTC. Then at least I wouldn't have fretted over what to do with my life.

Maybe a government job? Research? A newspaper? Forget it. Even if I knew what I wanted, those bastards would still be out there, those interviewers, just waiting to expose the peach-fuzzed imposter. *Ha! You expect me to hire an empty vessel like you? Let's see here...a useless degree, experience in food service...you got you some grades, boy, but what can you do besides fool 'em on a midterm?*

By late April I was swooning out of control. I even looked forward to the carefree solace of the supermarket, where I sometimes caught myself addressing startled shoppers. One afternoon in my apartment, chewing food I couldn't taste, I searched my jumbled skull for a pleasant memory, a soothing thought, anything that might get me through a sandwich...

I remembered the moment I first saw a shrimper slog its lonely way home from the Gulf. The sea and sky beyond Brownsville had merged that day, hiding the horizon behind a giant gray gauze. The tide was following the boat in, and the breeze blew sticky and tart. I was alone on a fishing pier, tamed by a quart of cold Jax, drowsy in the familiar warmth of a Texas summer dusk.

The boat churned by, all rust and bow foam and frayed rope. Sea gulls were begging and swooping over the stern. The deckhand picked scraps of fish from his net and tossed them into the wake. Through the open cabin doors, cast against the seascape, stood the captain. He was an old man with both hands on the wheel, rolling with the swells while he sucked on a fat pipe. His face was hidden in a shadow, but his posture and the sway of his shoulders said he was making this trip for the uncounted thousandth time.

How I envied that old skipper his worn pipe, his easy footing, his command of the boat and the water. Not a molecule of self-doubt in him. He probably slept like a house cat and woke every morning without the slightest fear of failure.

Three years had passed since that moment, but I could still smell the salted creosote and hear the tide slapping against the piles. Slowly, I began to sense I was getting somewhere.

For me the water had always been an ally, a kind of sanctuary from life's aggressions. In my early days I scrambled to the creekbank near our house when the price of growing up seemed too high. As a teenager I often sought the warm refuge of Lake Worth under the stars. Life on land was just as pitiless when I came back, but the currents never failed to salve a wound or wash the mental tangles away.

For the first time in months I thought decisively: I would go to the coast and work on a fishing boat, live the simple life, plod through the post-graduate panic, determine what to do with the five-decade semester that loomed before me.

I was twenty-one years old, on the verge of the most important decisions of my life. What I needed was a larger body of water.

One

In the years that have passed since my pilgrimage to the coast, I am struck more and more by the tenuous underpinnings of life. Had my father not chanced to settle in Texas after the Korean war, had my mother not lost her first fiance in it—or even if she had conceived her child a month later or a month before—this collection of squiggles would never have found this page. In the same way I wonder how different I would be today had I aimed my car back to Fort Worth after college, or to San Francisco, New York, or any of the scores of other cities where my classmates chose to build their lives.

Instead, tied in the private knots that my mother might have prevented with a mere headache twenty-two years before, I stumbled into the town where Donna, the incomparable Donna, lived. Of course, I couldn't know it as I waved goodbye to Austin and all of its pleasant confusions, but I was on the verge of an entanglement that would forever change me, one that has delighted and haunted me ever since.

The first day of my adulthood was among the most fateful, not because I met Donna (who shuffled onstage the second day), but because I came upon two others who would do so much to frame my understanding of her. I am certain that if Knuckles Dupree or Bunny Hogner had never existed, or if I had come to know Donna without knowing them, everything would have been different. But things happened as they happened. Countless unrelated events came together in just a cer-

tain sequence, and I found myself facing choices and conse-
quences that would never go away.

The drawbridge emerged from the horizon just before
noon that day and rested briefly on my hood like a shiny new
ornament. The sun had already stilled the wind over
Galveston Bay and goaded the waterfront's stenches to a
rousing bloom. The tide was down, and on the roadbed a
black man and his tiny daughter were striving solemnly to
tempt crabs with a chicken neck. Everything about the
place—the rust, the bleached lumber, the riprap, the hand-let-
tered signs—was as rough and as beautiful as I remembered.

I had decided where to go almost as quickly as I decided
that I would go. About twenty-five miles south of Houston,
halfway to Galveston in fact, lie two small villages on the
banks of a channel fed by the bay. Adelia inhabits the northern side, and a city called Maxwell lies to the south. The narrow creek that divides them leads inland from the bay's
northwestern shore to Clear Lake, where thousands of yachts
sway indolently in elegant marinas.

In the summer of 1973, after a tourist stop at NASA a few
miles away, I had spent an afternoon in an Adelia beer joint
gazing at the Maxwell side. I was struck by the artless vigor of
both shores and by the sturdy drawbridge that joined them.

It was a constant presence, the bridge, one that dominated
the landscape and the lives of everyone in it. The bridge was
built to span the briny gap in the highway, but its effect was to
turn motorists into sweaty supplicants before the main masts
of the wealthy. Miles of backed-up, overheating cars meant
nothing: The massive hinges rose at the merest hint that
someone in Bermuda shorts wished to sail about the bay.

Sailboats were the masters of the drawbridge, but the
Maxwell and Adelia channel docks were not theirs. Those belonged to working shrimp and oyster boats, to the beer joints
that served them, to the fish houses and restaurants that
bought their harvests. Air on the bay side of the bridge was
alive with jukeboxes and the throat-chafing stench of fish out
of water. Its dock workers were shirtless and tough, with

sweaty pants tucked into rubber boots and wiry hair that bent away from the bay. The bridge, erected halfway between the bay and the lake, seemed to separate work from leisure, wages from capital, muscle from cellulite. I couldn't wait to immerse myself in the fevered, slippery-skinned wonders on the wrong side of the bridge.

The immediate plan was to make the rounds of the fish houses along the creek and find a shrimper in need of a deckhand. It wasn't the three-martini recruitment my father envisioned when he signed tuition checks, but the simple clarity of it all did wonders for my nerves. An obvious place to start was the Captain Borneo, the largest and most famous fish market on the channel. My adventure began there quietly, amid the muffled pops of oyster shells as my car rolled in from the road.

The Borneo was a wooden building propped up on stilts about four feet from the ground. It was recently painted white, but already its walls were rust-stained at the windows like a drunk with runny eyes. Two Mexican boys were kneeling among the stilts, teasing a desperate crab with a stick. On the top step of the porch, my shoulders tightened—the stink of a fish market was even angrier than I remembered. I braced myself and took the deepest breath my lungs could endure.

Cold air swept past as I stepped inside, and that took some of the bite off the smell. The shop was dark and spacious, with an L-shaped counter stocked with ice and a wide assortment of fish. Piles of shrimp, heads on and heads off, big shrimp and small, brown shrimp and white. Buckets of shucked oysters and scallops. Rows of redfish, trout, snapper, flounder. To the left on the floor was a long box clicking with clumsy crabs. All the fish were fresh and firm, in perfect condition, sending their stink to every crevice in the room.

A bored, black-haired woman with porcelain skin rose from her stool behind the counter. The flesh on her arms jiggled when she tapped out a cigarette and asked what she could sell me today.

"Actually," I said, "I'm looking for a job."

"Sorry, don't need nobody. Shoulda been in a couple days ago. He caught one of the Mexicans stealing and fired every man on the dock."

"I was hoping to find a shrimp boat."

"Ever worked a boat before?"

"No. I'm just out of college and—"

She raised a hand to hush me and turned to the back of the shop. I hadn't noticed the old man sitting there on an over-turned bucket.

"Hey, Knucks," the woman shouted, clearly enjoying herself. "We got us a college boy on his summer vacation. Says he wants to crew a boat."

She turned back and looked beyond me to the front door.

"You go talk to Knuckles, there. He's the man you need to see."

Courtesy compelled me to meet the old man, but I could feel my ears getting warm. He sat upright with his hands between his knees, holding two squat bottles of Lone Star. When he looked up and smiled I stopped short. He had one visible tooth, moist yellow eyes and a wrinkled face that was punished by the sun beyond the leathery stage.

"Hello," I said. "My name is Samuel Traynor. I'm trying to find a job on a shrimp boat."

I followed the deep lines from his chin to his forehead and back down again. I imagined fingertips trained in a special Braille could find in those furrows an epic tale of hangovers and rope burns, knife slashings and brutal labor.

"I've never done this kind of thing before," I said. "But I'll work hard. I'm sure I can learn quickly."

The old man raised one of his beer bottles and gazed vacantly at the ceiling as he drank—and I realized how he came by his name. Arthritis had given his hands the look of mangled claws. His fingers twisted unpredictably this way and that, and the knuckles were the size of walnuts. He tossed the bottle a few feet to a garbage can, then offered his hand to me.

"Chris Dupree," he said in a deep, warm voice. "Most peoples call me Knuckles."

I imagined him crushing my hand like a fresh Saltine, but he hardly clasped at all. I learned later the arthritis wouldn't let him. The skin on his fingers felt coarse and lifeless, as though a welder's glove was draped over the bones with no meat to fill it out.

"Allus works by myself," he said.

I suppressed a whoop of relief that I wouldn't be confined to a boat with that face and those hands.

"Allus have worked by myself. Allus will, too."

"Would you know if anyone else is looking for a deckhand?"

Knuckles took another drink and thought carefully.

"Onliest time I ever worked with somebody else was my second wife. Didn't last too long, neither. She jumped off the second day and swam all the way to a channel marker till somebody come by and pick her up.

"That was the last time I saw her, flappin' in the water like a wormy hound. She took up with the sumbitch that fished her out."

I looked toward the counter. The black-haired woman turned quickly to conceal a laugh.

"See, she didn't know what you got to know if you're gonna be a deck hand: The captain, he's the boss. You don't got to know much, but you got to know that foreways and backwards."

A long pause.

"She didn't."

I took a deep breath and tried again.

"Well, I was wondering if you knew anyone around here looking for a deck hand."

"Deck hand, eh? You wants you a job?"

"Yessir."

"They's a bait house on the Maxwell side, and the boy who runs it wants it painted up. He was looking for somebody on account of he fell off a ladder once and tore up his back. He don't get on no ladders ever since."

I started edging for the door.

"Where you goin'?" Knuckles rose from the bucket. "I thought you was wanting you a job."

He killed what was left of the second bottle and tossed it in the can. I was back to the counter now, and the woman could see I was stricken.

"Don't get the wrong idea," she said under her breath. "Knucks ain't half as crazy as he looks."

Half as crazy as that man looked left plenty of room for crazy. I'd been a full-fledged adult for all of five minutes, and already my life was in the enormous hands of a guy called Knuckles.

It probably took him only seconds to cross the room, but it seemed an afternoon. He had to be at least sixty, but his step possessed some of the style of a strutting pimp: loose wrists, palms facing the floor, his long body angled forward from the butt. He wore brown work pants and a plaid cotton shirt, both of them lined with salt patterns formed by weeks of perspiration.

Then I saw the green tattoo. A naked Oriental woman, faded with age and almost hidden by his tan, squatted on his left forearm with her arms wrapped seductively around her head. I have never seen such an explicit tattoo, and the image was especially jarring next to his scraggy face. I knew he hadn't touched a woman in years.

"If you really think you wanna be a deck hand," he sighed, "c'mon, I'll show you where to go."

Outside Knuckles hung by one arm from a corner post and squinted into the sun.

"Gonna be a hot one," he said. "Just as well I didn't go out, on account of I lost my hat and that sun woulda burned me right up."

He raised a hand in the direction of the creek, his fingers pointing in five different directions.

"Over there, on the Maxwell side. See that metal building with the fuel pumps on the dock?"

I shielded my eyes and found it. Two stories, beige walls, a faded sign over the dock: Tina's Marina, All the Beer and Diesel You Can Drink.

"Go tell 'em what you want. That's where most boats gets their fuel. Captains usual put the word out there when they want some help."

Tina's Marina was only a few feet from Tony Red's, the swank seafood restaurant with the stunning view and the statewide reputation. It was striking to see a weather-beaten shrimper hangout within spitting distance of the place.

I wasn't sure, but I guessed Knuckles was telling the truth. I reached impulsively for his hand.

"Yeah, good luck," he said. Then he laughed and shook his head. "With them baby-butt hands, you gonna need it."

I stared down at my palms and felt a sudden weakness. Never before had they seemed so pudgy and pink. When I finally looked up again, Knuckles Dupree was gone.

*   *   *

I drove past Maxwell's weary beer joints and white parking lots until my eyes fell upon a giant mermaid, the centerpiece of a mural adorning the marina's corrugated wall. An inscription near the roof read, "My name is Tina. This here's my marina."

Cast as she was against faded lumber and tilted pilings, Tina was a beautiful, almost animate creature. Her arms rose elegantly to support trays of sweaty beer cans, and her eyes suggested carnal desire for every driver gazing up from the dust. Whoever created Tina had little use for coyness or subtle brush strokes. Golden hair cascaded down her back, and her breasts drooped over the landscape like fleshy breadfruit— each crowned with erect, two-inch nipples. The proprietors of Tony Red's must have been feverish the day they encountered those rosebuds.

I parked near Tina's dorsal region and heard the rhythmic buzz of a jukebox behind her. To the right was a covered wooden deck with folding chairs and formica tables. To the left stood a long single-story building with two doors. One door, heavily padlocked, led to a walk-in freezer. The other had "Office" stenciled above a rusty mail slot.

There was a sudden, loud crash in the bar. The door burst open, with a short man pushing at the knob until it slammed into Tina's tail. He closed the door with a ceremonial flourish and started down the stairs, pointedly ignoring the handrail. On the bottom step he bent to tie a loose shoelace and completed a perfect somersault onto the jagged shells.

"Oh, yes," he said, scanning the wispy clouds. "That does feel nice."

I offered my hands.

"That won't be necessary, young man. I'm quite fine."

He rose to one knee with a grunt and then flopped to the seat of his pants.

"It would appear I have compromised my motor functions. Perhaps I should set aside my pride and accept your assistance."

I brushed at the back of his shirt and noticed a stethoscope dangling from his neck. He focused on a point just below my chin and exhaled a roiling vat of hops.

"I believe I have regained my equilibrium," he said. "Perhaps one day our respective conditions will be such that I can return the favor." He headed for the asphalt with his arms spread for balance. When he disappeared around the office there was a crash of garbage cans and an ebullient," Oh, yes, ye-es."

I climbed the wooden steps to the office and took a deep breath as I opened the door. The air inside smelled like a wet ashtray—the docks were a Beverly Hills flower shop in comparison. The woman behind the counter raised a thick, tapered finger to say she would be off the phone soon. She reached for a cigarette behind her desk, the movement unveiling every inch of her vast, white thighs. She rearranged her hem calmly and tossed a match, still burning, into a fruit bowl filled with hundreds of purple-stained butts.

Bunny Hogner, the nameplate said. She studied me for a moment, then hung up without a word.

"What can I do ya for?"

There was a tobacco shred on her tongue, and she picked it

away with a lavender fingernail. I gave my name and said I'd heard this was the place to find a shrimp boat. She tilted her head and sniffed.

"Sure enough, honey. That's what they say."

I stared at her lipstick for a few awkward seconds. She might have had a bawdy appeal during the Eisenhower years, but too many Winstons and too much paper-bagged booze had given her face a fleshy snarl.

"You don't look like no deck hand."

"You're right," I said quickly. "But I'm eager to learn and willing to work."

"I can tell you're not from around here. What kind of trouble you in, honey?"

There wasn't enough daylight left to address that question fully, so I repeated what I'd said at the Captain Borneo.

"So, a college boy. We don't get too many of those. You gonna give your teacher a report: How I spent my summer as a real live shrimper?"

It occurred to me that already two people had assumed I would return to school in the fall—and I realized that misunderstanding flattered me more than the truth.

"No ma'am. Just want a job. Anyone need a deck hand?"

Her teeth were wet and on edge, an expression born of a thousand midnights in seedy bars. I imagined a portrait of her, framed by stacked beer cases and clouds of stubborn smoke. She folded her arms beneath her breasts and drew them upward.

"I wouldn't know about no deck hands, honey. You'll never catch me in that goddamn place. I just tend the books and pay the vendors out here. Donna's the one they talk to—the day-shift bar girl."

I thanked her and turned for what now seemed fresh air outside.

"You won't find her in there, honey. Donna's off, same as every Monday. You'll have to catch her in the morning."

I must have allowed too much disappointment onto my face, because Bunny sat up and tamped out her cigarette.

"You poor little rascal," she said sweetly. "Things ain't exactly clicking for you, are they?"

I shrugged and felt vaguely relieved.

"Tell you what, then. I expect you need a place to stay. Rodney Gene—he's the guy that owns this dump—he built a little room over the bar for the dock hand. Whoever that is gets it free, but we ain't had a dock hand in a week. How about you take it tonight, free of charge?

"Of course, you can have it long as you want—if you take the job. Hey, college, wanna be a dock hand?"

"Thanks, but I came to work on a boat."

Bunny leaned forward and lowered her voice.

"Listen up, sonny boy. These people, they'll tie a guy like you up in knots. It's hard work and a dirty life on that water. Meant for hard and dirty people, not decent folk.

"Can I tell you something, honey? I expect I can. It's a whole different class from you and me. They're low-lifes in there, schemers—bums is what they are. That's why I spend all my time right here in this office. I don't want to get mixed up in their shit and wind up with a knife down my throat.

"Maybe it's just as well you don't get messed up in no shrimping. I'd hate to see a nice boy get ruined."

"Thanks," I finally said, my scalp tingling. "But I came here to work on a shrimp boat. It's very important that I follow through on that."

Bunny sighed and reached for another cigarette. "All right, all right. At least I did my good deed for the day."

I reached numbly for the door and heard her tell me to wait.

"Look, I'll make you a deal. Boat jobs don't grow on trees, you know. You might sit around a couple of weeks before you find something. If you work on the dock in the meantime, it'll give you a job and a roof until you finally get yourself killed."

I started to say no, but the idea made sense. I wouldn't have to commit to a room until I knew where my boat was docked, and I'd have an immediate income. Best of all, I would be above the marina, the perfect place to taste life on the waterfront.

"Well, yes. I think I'd appreciate that very much."

"Strike up the goddamn band," Bunny sighed. She pulled a handful of keys from a drawer and labored out of her chair. "You follow me. It's gonna be hot as hell up there. The air ain't been on in a week."

Bunny's high-heeled sandals weren't built with oyster shell in mind, and on the parking lot she grabbed my shoulder to steady herself. We both felt it flinch.

"Don't worry, honey. I don't bite unless I'm asked."

I gave Bunny's sandals a head start on the stairs. Her phlegm-laden voice finally emerged from the doorway.

"You coming or not? I don't wanna burn up in this hell hole a second longer than I have to."

My new home was a plywood enclosure in the corner of a dusty attic. I walked past lumber, bar furniture, dim mounds of unidentifiable junk, and then almost skipped with joy at what I saw. The room had a giant window overlooking the fuel dock, with an unobstructed view of the channel, the bridge, and the gray-green expanse of Galveston Bay. I would awaken in the morning to the vista that made Tony Red's famous. Shrimpers and their rigging, speed boats, bikinis on fifty-foot yachts—it would all pass below me like a coronation parade.

The room itself was actually a squalid little place, with a lumpy bed that smelled vaguely of gasoline. The only other furniture was a small chest of drawers, a hot plate, an apartment refrigerator and a plastic shower stall. Bunny pointed to the rumpled linen on the bed and said I should wash it unless I enjoyed sleeping on roach turds.

"Take the afternoon to get settled, Sam. You start work tomorrow morning at six. Be downstairs when Donna opens the place, and she'll tell you what to do."

I was staring out the window when Bunny walked up from behind and pinched my cheek between two sweaty fingers.

"A word to the wise, kiddo. You need to watch out for that Donna, you hear?"

The message eventually reached me, but before I could ask what she meant Bunny had tossed the keys on the dresser and left.

A deep horn sounded at the drawbridge. I crawled onto the bed and watched the jaws ascend slowly until a teak-trimmed ketch slipped under the gate. A man in a polo shirt stood at the wheel, smiling easily while a tanned woman and two young girls tugged at the sails. The boat motored past the Captain Borneo, where a shrimp boat was unloading its boxes and baskets.

The boats took no notice of one another, but they were framed together in my second-story window, each in its own way perfect, all vigor and elegance. And, with everything spread out before me, they were mine...all mine.

Two

Tuesday began with the squeak of a faucet and muffled commotion on the dock. During the night I had opened the window to feel even closer to the bay, but as my head cleared in the darkness it was obvious I had only brought myself nearer the diesel pump.

"OK, pretty misses, off you go."

It was a woman's voice, insistent yet softened by a lisp. I couldn't see anyone outside.

"Don't sit there like a queen. I'm trying to save your life."

Nobody answered, and I felt my heart break into a trot. The clock said five twenty-nine—the alarm would explode in less than a minute. I reached for it and stood quietly near the window.

"I mean it now. Off, or else."

There was a blast from a water hose, then a small splash in the channel, and I began to breathe again. Someone was waging battle with a piece of trash.

I dressed without the light and stepped downstairs, where a woman was crouched over two crab traps near my door. At first, all I saw was a sleeveless blouse stretched tight across a muscled back. Then she stood, and for an instant I saw my grandmother poking around the kitchen for her dentures— a long glazed face, drawn in around a cratered mouth. But she took a vigorous step toward me, and my grandmother vanished.

"Hey, you're either a burglar or a new dock hand," she said. "I'm Donna."

I reached to greet her and brushed against an abdomen as tight as a gymnast's. She squeezed my hand and apologized for making it wet.

"Might wanna hose off," she said. "I'm backin' crabs, and I think I just gave you a handful of guts."

She stepped back to the traps and dragged one into the glare of the dock light. That stirred a clackety confusion among the prisoners inside.

"Like crab?" she said.

Her face was still hidden in the shadows. I admired the way her hips filled her jeans and said I didn't know.

"Well, you'll find out soon enough. Got about a dozen, and most of 'em is males."

She turned to the trap and used tongs to lift a giant crab to the dock. Her hair was swept back in a yellow-gray pony tail that seemed to gather rays from the light.

"Some people think you oughta boil a crab with his shell on, but they don't pick up as much flavor that way. If you ask me, it's a lot better to clean 'em first."

I was distracted by the curious quality of her voice. Her lisp was cheerful, yet somehow daunting.

"Don't think I got your name," she said.

"Sam Traynor. Bunny told me I should see you."

Donna stiffened for an instant, then pulled an ice pick from a dock piling.

"Two things you gotta remember when you're backin' a crab, Sam." Whatever bothered her about Bunny was forgotten. She seemed pleased by the chance to share her skill. "First, stay away from his claws, or he'll really put the hurt on you. Second, poke him in the head so you can get at his shell."

Donna lowered herself to one knee and motioned me forward. Her flat sandals and unbrassiered breasts made her seem almost like a campus apparition.

"See, just hold him against the deck with the tongs. Then take something sharp and *jam* it right down behind his lips."

Clear liquid oozed from the crab's shell toward its eyes. Donna released the tongs, and the crab lurched awkwardly in front of us.

"That mushes up his brain, so he don't know where he's aiming his claws. He's pretty mad, but he can't hit nothing but air."

The crab stumbled in an clumsy circle, and I took a step back. Donna dabbed at her forehead.

"I'm sorry," she murmured. "You ain't been around the water much, have you?"

"No—yes—I mean, I just never saw that before."

"You probably think I'm awful, then. I guess this looks pretty rough the first time."

"No," I blurted. "I've cleaned a lot, well, quite a few fish. I'm just not used to seeing them fight back."

"Well, crabs'll eat you up if you let 'em. I saw a kid forget to poke a crab once, and it took the end of his pinky finger off. You just can't back a crab, without you poke him first."

She reached for the shell from behind.

"Once you got him poked, it's easy. Just grab him by the legs and *crrrack*, his back tears right off." The crab's intestines glistened under the dock light, its legs and pinchers jerking wildly. "That orange blob behind his lips, that's his brains. Just *poke* it real quick with your finger, and it's over."

Donna picked up the limp shell and hosed away the entrails. Soon nothing was left but a clean white delicacy.

"How 'bout it, Sam. Give it a go?"

It was the last thing I wanted to try at that moment, but when Donna handed me the tongs I felt obliged. I lifted an angry specimen to the dock, reached for the ice pick, and neglected the tongs just long enough to set the crab free. I heard a throaty laugh behind me.

"Fight him, Sam, fight him! Don't let him get away!"

The crab was sidestepping across the dock to freedom. I stumbled after it and realized I had nothing to use but the ice pick.

"You'll need these," I heard Donna say. But the crab was

already at the edge of the dock. I reached down to shoo it back, and it lashed out at my wrist. The world began to fall away.

"Here, grab me!" Donna said. I reached for her hand, looked up into the light, and felt suddenly weightless...the crab landed on me and danced on my chest until the impact of the water took us apart. The bay had a pleasant warmth.

"Say. Say! You all right?"

It was a plaintive voice, wading slowly across the vast distance between the dry and the submerged. There was nothing in the glare above me now but the outline of a delicious female form.

"Oh, Lord. Tell me you're okay."

I coughed on a noseful of brine and said I would pull through. I couldn't reconcile Donna's body with her face. Was that what Bunny meant?

"There's kind of a ladder by the ice locker. It's your easiest way out, if you can just kinda swim around to here."

The water was scummed with the ugly residues of the fuel dock, and I couldn't wait to get out. I waved at her silhouette and splashed around the pilings, careful not to touch anything and praying my feet wouldn't find the bottom. Finally there was the damp glint of the ladder and Donna reaching down from the shadows.

"I feel terrible about this." She clasped my arm. "Thought I had you for a minute, but you got away."

I splashed onto the dock and tried to cut my losses. "Well, I think my qualifications speak for themselves."

Donna laughed and in a sudden rush of euphoria threw her arms around me.

"I love it, Sam! That's the spirit!"

I felt the pleasant pressure of her breasts and prayed for a chance to see her dampened shirt under the dock light. Donna pressed her face hard into my chest, then backed away to give me a playful punch. I should have been able to see her at last, but the salt was still stinging my eyes.

"Don't worry, I ain't jumping your bones, Sam. It's just

nice to have a guy around here who can laugh at himself."

"Comes naturally," I said. "I keep myself in stitches."

Donna laughed again and tapped at the dampness on her clothes. Then she reached out with both hands to brush hair from my face. Her hands lingered longer than necessary, and I felt the first tingles of arousal.

"You probably think I'm crazy, Sam. But seeing you come out of the water like that—it reminded me of something I ain't thought about in years."

"I can jump back in if you'd like."

"You would, wouldn't you?" She slipped her arm across the small of my back and pointed me toward my door. "Tell you what, Sam. Let me go ahead and finish these crabs. You'd better rinse off and find some dry clothes."

I thanked her and climbed the stairs. I wasn't quite up to facing myself in the mirror, so I peeled in the darkness and listened to the *crrrack* of crab backs in the stale air outside.

*   *   *

The sun was only moments away when I stepped onto the dock again. A shrimp boat was drifting down the channel, its drowsy deckhand occupied with preparations for the day. The boat slip near my door was littered with bobbing crab shells, and the traps were already baited under the dock to collect another meal. Donna was filling the coffee maker when I bounded in like a hungry Bible salesman.

"Dry as a bone," I said. "Always nice to start the day with a bracing plunge."

Donna spun around with an angelic smile. There was not a tooth in her head.

"Here," she said, pointing to a barstool. "Have a seat and tell me all about my new dock hand."

It took only an instant to see past her unfortunate mouth. Donna was blessed with a stunning, square-jawed beauty that glowed with health and vigor. Still, she seemed well into middle age, and I couldn't believe this was the sexy athlete I

had seen on the dock. But the glorious turns of her damp
blouse assured me it was.

"I wasn't expecting no hand this morning, but it's good to
see ya."

More than anything it was her mouth, her tender peach of
a mouth, that aged her. It had the look of an accident, and a
recent one at that. The lines that spread from her lips seemed
shallow and impermanent, as though her cheeks were still
unsure about where to rest.

"I should tell you why I'm here," I said. "I'm looking for a
shrimp boat, and Bunny said you'd know who needed a
hand. She told me I could work here until something came
up."

The mention of Bunny's name changed the alignment of
Donna's gums. She glanced at me with a cool, tight-pupiled
wariness, and I imagined she saw the world as a wolf
would—an overbright landscape of fleeting threats and pleasures.

"You and Bunny friends?" she said.

"Met her yesterday. I'm out of college, and I need the
work."

Donna's eyes began to soften.

"College, huh? You sure you want to work a shrimp boat?"

"I know I'm green, but I'm willing. I'll get it done if somebody will just give me a chance."

"What you want—bay boat or gulf boat?" Her eyes moved
over me quickly, and I had the sinking feeling I was being regarded by a superior intelligence.

"Sorry, I don't know the difference."

"Well, bay boats go out in the morning and come back every night. Gulf boats go offshore and stay days at a time."

"I really don't know. Which would be better for me?"

She studied my torso for a moment and said bay boat.
There was no objection I could righteously raise, but I had just
been judged and found wanting.

"Bay boat's better for people who haven't been out," she
added mercifully. "That way if you don't like the work, or

you're the kind that gets seasick, you can quit in a hurry. Otherwise you might spend a week hanging over a rail."

Donna had let me down gently, but I had the unmistakable sense she thought I should get back in the car while I still had a chance. Maybe if I had been strong enough to face myself in those days, I would have done it.

"Bay boat," I said. "A bay boat sounds right."

She looked at me without speaking, and I began to stare back like a stock-still fawn. Her face seemed to reflect everything inside me—months of worry, guilty dread, frantic uncertainty. Somehow she had surveyed my soul and felt every emotion hidden there.

"All right, Sam." Donna seemed embarrassed by the almost psychic liberties she had taken. "Soon's I hear of something, you'll be the first to know." She found a rag and started wiping the counter between us. "Meantime, you're gonna like it here. If you take a shine to the water and shrimping and all, this is the place to be—even better than a boat, if you ask me."

I heard a door open and turned to see a white-headed little girl emerge from the restroom pulling up her shorts. She spun around modestly when she saw me, exposing a pair of plump little cheeks as she struggled with her elastic waistband.

"That's Sharlene," Donna said. "She's a pistol, that one."

The girl looked coyly over her shoulder.

"So," I said, relieved that the focus of the conversation had shifted from me. "It's Sharlene the Pistol, is it?" I bowed toward her, and she giggled. "And how old a woman are you, Miss Pistol?"

"Two!" she said proudly.

"Then you know how to talk?"

"Two!"

Donna laughed. "That's her favorite word," she said, "on account of it's her only word."

"Two, huh?"

"Two!"

Sharlene hugged herself and watched me watch her. She had a broad Nordic face and hair that rested in silky ringlets about her neck. She was a gorgeous waif with big round eyes and a tiny nose.

"Is she yours?" I wondered aloud.

"That would be a stunner, wouldn't it, Sam?"

I felt myself blanch, but Donna's grin showed she wasn't offended.

"No, she ain't mine, but then again she is. Her momma couldn't handle being a momma, so Sharlene wound up with me. She's in here today because her babysitter has to go to the foot doctor."

The girl ran to Donna and hid behind her jeans.

"Yeah, you're a bashful one," Donna said. "About as bashful as a stripper, you are."

Sharlene showed her face long enough to extend a pink, pointed tongue. Donna responded with the most labial raspberry I have ever seen.

"Alright, squirt, that's enough foolishness for one morning. I want you to say hello to Sam, here. He's our new dockhand."

She withdrew her tongue and looked up at me like a wary card player.

"Go on," Donna said, urging her out from behind her knees. "Tell Sam how happy we are to have him."

Trying to coax her, I bent down and offered my hand. Sharlene stepped slowly forward, her fists covering a bashful smile, and touched my palm with an index finger. "Two," she said.

"Sharlene, I'm pleased to meet you, too."

"Two?" she asked.

"Too."

The answer seemed to satisfy her. She sighed dramatically and glanced about for a diversion, settling at last on a stack of beer coasters near the register. Donna and I watched her take two handfuls to a nearby table, where she arranged them in a rectangular pattern before hurrying back to the register.

"Two," she told Donna purposefully.

"Oh, oh yeah." Donna reached behind the coffee maker

and pulled out a small spatula, which Sharlene used to flip the coasters like flapjacks on a griddle. Then she stacked three on a napkin and handed them to me.

"Well, congratulations, Sam. She doesn't usually cook for somebody unless she's known them awhile."

"Thank you, Sharlene. Thank you very much." I started to set the coasters on the bar, but her keen interest in how I received them moved me to take a healthy bite.

"Delicious!" I declared. "Such flavor! Such texture!"

Sharlene shrieked a delirious two and slapped her tiny palms together. Then she turned back to the table to tend her flapjacks before they burned.

*　　*　　*

Finally I thought to ask for my chores, and Donna sounded almost apologetic when she said I should spray the night's salty residues from the windows and patio furniture. Across the channel at the Captain Borneo, the fish woman in the stretch pants was dumping a bucket of water into the creek. She saw me and raised a congratulatory fist in the air. Up the creek, I could hear a shrimper start his engine and rumble slowly from a slip. Next door to the marina, Tony Red's was as empty as a ghost ship, with the morning sun turning its tablecloths into fluorescent lilies.

The marina door slammed, and through the windows I could see Knuckles riding his stiff-backed pimp strut to the bar. He eased onto a stool and lit a cigarette while Donna reached for the coffee, a routine honed by hundreds of repetitions. Donna poured a cup and folded her forearms on the bar only inches from his, waiting for his first pronouncements of the day.

That little gesture, warming up affectionately to a visage like Knuckles, made me think again of Bunny's warning. Yet there was nothing threatening in the picture I saw, no irony in Donna's smile, nothing forced. She didn't even seem to be thinking ahead to her chores or to what she would say next.

She was just savoring a moment with another human being, brightening the morning of an unfortunate who probably hadn't touched a woman in years. Bunny had to be wrong.

In the flat light of the bar, Donna's hair was a soft blend of gold, white and metallic gray, and her pony tail gave her forehead a flattering breadth. She moved out to straighten some chairs, shuffling in quick steps like a ten-year-old hurrying to her room with a friend. Her face was actually quite smooth, with most of the wrinkles confined to the busy contours around her mouth. She licked her bottom lip as she worked and never attempted to hide her toothlessness. Surely no woman with such an acute awareness could fail to notice such a defect, even in herself. Yet it seemed not to bother her, and she had taken a very public job despite it.

Was it her figure, or her lovely eyes, that made it so easy to look past her only flaw? Was it her magnetic grace, or the courage that moved her to greet a stranger on a darkened dock? Surely it was all of that and more, but most of all it was this: Donna had an air of assurance, a complete self-possession that I could only dream of for myself. And at that moment in my life, nothing could have been more appealing in a woman, or a man.

Donna moved back to the bar, and I turned to the sound of another engine up by the bridge. It was a sailboat, steered by a bald man whose eyes never veered from the path before him. That seemed strange, because the waterfront was a treasure of peculiar sights. Then it came to me: He was ignoring the docks the way mailmen ignore loose dogs to keep them away. He was on the wrong side of the bridge now, worried that someone, some snot-covered demon of the waterfront, was leering at him and deciding where to fling his jagged blade.

There was no one on the docks then but me. I entertained the thought that it was my stare he was trying to avoid. I hitched my pants and spat, and I could have sworn my palms were beginning to toughen. For the first time I sensed I was on the inside of this place looking out.

Back in the bar, Donna was still listening to Knuckles. I wondered what the sailor would think of this toothless barmaid with the raw eyes. It was obvious that Donna could see a lot—would she see the discomfort in his face? Had she seen it in mine? Then I realized that questions like those wouldn't have occurred to me if I had seen Donna as Rodney Gene did when he hired her, or as Knuckles did from behind his coffee cup. I had fled to Maxwell with the wild and stupid optimism of the desperate, but now I was alone on a dock with a garden hose in my hand, still very much on the outside looking in.

* * *

All morning the creek was busy with shrimp boats aimed at the sun in random ones and twos. The boats carried powerful and impressive men who moved with unaffected ease, like satisfied celebrities. Life seemed more vivid on those boats, more direct, and every man aboard them radiated a sense of clear and uncompromised purpose. I couldn't wait for my chance to be out there with them, hidden among the swells on the wet plain to Galveston.

That is not to say the marina was an unpleasant place. For a romantic young man with an eye to the sea, Tina's was by far the best duty the shore had to offer. The marina was free of the brutal drudgery of the fish house, and the building looked just disgusting enough to keep most Bermuda shorts away.

There were twenty tables in Tina's, with half as many on the patio. Near the front door stood a pool table. Behind it was a juke box, elevated on cinder blocks to keep it above the tide during storms. The window banks gave a view of the busy creek, Tony Red's, and the bay beyond. Every window was framed with faded lace curtains stiffened by years of dust and inattention. Their faded cheer gave the room a melancholy cast, at least to eyes that hadn't lost sight of them through daily habit.

The inventory behind the bar was a random sampling of potato chips, starter fluid, motor oil, packaged sandwiches, fuel filters, cupcakes. Everything was piled casually on a counter, oil cans nestled against food products, all of it dulled by heavy brown grime. Until the air conditioners took effect in the mornings, the dominant impression was of mildew clinging desperately to life.

Despite the dirt and decay, I sensed that this had once been a flashier building, a place surrounded by cabin cruisers owned by sports who smirked like Robert Wagner. Certainly the curtains had been lovely once, and there must have been a time when the gray dock was new and the bar was free of shell dust.

*   *   *

Sharlene spent much of the morning following me on my beer runs to the ice locker, and she had fun trying to catch our frozen breaths with her hands. She was just a baby of two, but I was struck by the grown-up, sensual grace of her ears. They were pierced and adorned with tiny pearls, the lobes curving gently with just the perfect hint of flesh. In the ice locker they took on the aspect of rose petals. Her parents, whoever they were, must have been handsome creatures.

There was one unsettling moment, however. I was lifting a case of Schlitz when Sharlene edged so close I lost my balance. I dropped the case and avoided her, but she shrieked in terror, then cowered as I reached out to assure her. When it became clear I did not intend to hit her, she extended her left hand and struck the back of it with her right, then again, the pain shining in her eyes, until I embraced her to make her stop.

"What's the matter?" I whispered near her perfect ear. "Why would you want to hurt yourself?"

"Two," she whimpered, as if I has missed some large, obvious point. I kissed her reddened hand and soothed her until eventually she drifted to another distraction among the beer stacks.

*   *   *

During the next few hours Donna introduced me to the joys of boiled crab and the easy rituals involved in running a marina. We reviewed the cash register, the fuel meters, the juke box volume control. By ten o'clock I was ready to run the place myself, and I soon got the chance. Just before noon, Donna went to Bunny's office for some credit card slips. Sharlene was sitting in front of me on the bar, restacking her pile of beer coasters, when a stocky Mexican man opened the door. He was so thrilled to see me he stopped combing his hair.

"Well, hello," he said expansively. "I'm Leo, Leo Sanchez. Let me guess—you're the new dock hand."

He ignored Sharlene and reached across the bar to shake hands. She suddenly seemed to be scowling at her coasters.

"So," he said, tugging at a pair of bright red pants, "where's Donna this morning?" He was delighted when I said she'd be back any second.

"She's already got you running things by yourself, I see. I'm sure she's glad to get you. Donna ain't even had a lunch break for almost a week now."

He was smiling so broadly I could see glistening white molars. It occurred to me that Donna could have used some of that enamel.

"Well, Sam, I'll take the usual. For me that's a can of Schlitz and a plastic drinking cup." He took it to the nearest window table and winked at me as he poured.

"So, you've already figured out the register and all, is that it? Attaboy, Sam. Last boy they had in here couldn't find his ass with both hands."

Donna opened the door and saw Leo, then looked quickly at me.

"Hey," she said, gazing halfway between us. She shuffled toward Leo's table and sat with her back toward me. Sharlene and I watched them talk quietly for several minutes. Leo, so ebullient when we met, was suddenly stern. He seemed to be trying to convince Donna of something, and he was running out of patience.

Eventually they fell silent. Donna jumped in her chair when I walked up from behind.

"Need another beer?" I said.

Leo grunted and shook his head once. I asked Donna if she wanted anything, and she said no without looking back. When I returned to the bar, Sharlene took up her coasters again and started handing them to me one by one. She counted aloud, assigning each, of course, the number two. Donna and Leo were staring vacantly at different phantoms, and I began to wonder about this strange couple, if that was what they were. They never touched, and Donna had approached him with casual courtesy. Then why the whispers?

Moments later Donna stood and pulled her purse from behind the register. She glanced quickly at my chin.

"Got a couple of errands," she said. "I'll be back in about a half hour, and then you can take your lunch break. If you need anything, Bunny's number is on the phone. Fair enough?"

Of course it was. Sharlene reached up with both arms, expecting to be lifted, but Donna leaned over and kissed her lightly on the lips.

"You keep an eye on Sam, OK?"

Sharlene looked puzzled at first, then nodded happily.

"Jaquita's probably gonna pick you up before I get back," Donna said, "so give me enough sugar to last the until this afternoon."

Sharlene blew kisses with both hands and gurgled a euphoric "Two!" Donna waved goodbye without looking at Leo and shuffled out into the heat. Leo turned to look at the bay, spinning his empty beer can before him. I asked again if he wanted another.

"No thanks, Sam." He stretched his neck awkwardly, then sighed. "Guess I'll just shove off."

It had been a strange episode, but I didn't have time to think about it. On his way out, Leo handed the door to a rowdy construction crew, whose two-fisted devotion to Schlitz and pork rinds kept me running until Donna came back.

*   *   *

On my way back from lunch at a nearby burger stand I passed Sharlene on the road leading to Tina's. She was standing on the front seat of a car driven by her babysitter, feasting on a hot dog which she dropped the moment she saw me. We waved furiously at one another, and I heard an excited "two" through our open windows before we sped our separate ways.

Then I walked into the bar to find Donna, alone, in a coughing fit near the register. She looked up with red panic on her face, and her knees suddenly buckled. As she fell, her hand sent remnants of a hot dog bun flying, and I realized she was choking on a piece of food.

I ran over and knelt helplessly beside her. She stopped coughing—not enough breath—and grabbed for my arm, but she couldn't make the connection. I took her hand and watched her face grow redder and redder.

"Jesus, what should I do?"

Donna tried to say something but only coughed again. For some reason I decided to get her on her feet. She couldn't stand, so I reached under her ribs to lift her—and it popped out, a marble-size piece of hot dog that looked like a chunk of her lung. Just that fast, just that accidentally, Donna was safe.

Before I could say anything she pulled me down behind her, gasping and shivering, and we both felt the same joyous terror. Just as I realized my fingers were still pressed deep into her breasts, she crossed her hands over mine so they would stay there. Donna rocked slowly in my arms, her firm back flexing against me, and for the first time I saw the thin white scar that traced her left jawline from ear to chin. It occurred to me at that moment, with her face angled away and mine resting in her hair, that there was nothing, save her mouth, that aged her.

"You saved me," she said. "I can't believe it. If you'd been one minute later, I'd have strangled on the floor of a goddamn beer joint."

I cleared my voice and asked her not to think about it. I was a lucky hero who had never heard of Heimlich, and I felt more embarrassed than proud.

Donna rested her head against my shoulder and began to cry.

"It's my goddamn teeth," she said, still short of breath. "If I had some teeth to chew with, it wouldn't have happened."

Without thinking, I asked why she didn't wear dentures.

"I wish to hell I did." She began to fidget. "I used to have 'em, and I was gonna have 'em, but..."

Donna straightened suddenly and reached for her hair. I wouldn't have thought it possible before, but she seemed self-conscious.

"That's a long, terrible story, Sam. Somebody like you wouldn't understand."

"Somebody like me?"

"Well, you know, a college boy and all. People like you don't understand about people like me."

Let it pass, I thought. *She's been through enough.*

"Thanks," I heard myself say. "You'd think I was a complete jerk if I said that to you."

Donna's turned toward me, and her gray eyes narrowed.

"I mean it, now. You're a nice boy and you just did a nice thing. But you forget about the other—understand?"

I looked away, and we both began the discreet motions necessary to stand again. I brought Donna some water, dampened a fresh cloth for her face, and set about acting as though the incident hadn't bothered me at all.

Three

By mid-afternoon Donna and I had lost the taste of adrenaline, and I was preoccupied with competing memories—Donna's taut breasts in my hands, and her flinty expression when she told me to mind my own business. Yet she had regained her easy grace within seconds and spent much of the day telling customers how her new hero saved her life.

I was outside, repairing a loose cleat on the dock, when the wind began to gust. I felt a firm grip on my shoulder and looked up to see Donna pointing at a dark cloud bank rolling in from the Gulf.

"Better top off the coolers," she said. "We're in for a rough spell."

"Rain?"

"Yeah, but that ain't the trouble. Look at the water."

Out on the black horizon, shrimpers were popping up like shooting gallery ducks.

"They're all trying to outrun the storm," she lisped. "Might make it if they're lucky, but they ain't gonna stay dry. They always think they can get in thirty more minutes of draggin' before the blow, but they forget everybody else is thinkin' the same thing. Then the fish houses get more crowded than Houston.

"So let's buckle up, Sam. They had to quit early, they're gonna be wet, and most of 'em are gonna wind up here."

Within half an hour the sky was pouring on rows of boats

tied beam-to-beam at the docks. The rain drove hard against our windows and transformed everything outside into a gray blur. Between gusts I could see white deck boots scurrying about at the Captan Borneo. Eventually the rain slowed to a trickle, and the sky behind the storm began to shine again. Donna laughed that everyone had cut his day short to avoid a 20-minute shower. A few boats headed back out, but most of the fleet chose to accept the gift.

Before long the bar was throbbing with the masters of the waterfront. They were tired and sore-muscled, with the smell of their catches still sharp on their skin. They walked in like hulking gods, serenely careless, their wet boots clomping heavily across the floor. Every one of them—even the old and the stooped—was a sturdy monument of pride. This bar, this town, this bay, belonged to no one else.

They gathered in random threes and fours and spoke in vague, elliptical spurts. "Hell," someone grumbled at a window table, "it's gettin' tough for a man to make a livin' out there."

Pronouncements like that would prompt everyone within earshot to bob his head solemnly.

"Fuckin' bay's about had it."

Another round of head bobs.

It would take me too long to learn it, but effusive talk on the waterfront was evidence of weakness, stupidity, a fatal lack of self-possession. Anyone foolish enough to report a heavy catch would find a welcoming party at his spot the next morning. Lies and comic boasts were the verbal currency. Dockside bars were filled with men who took offense at any ardently voiced opinion, be the subject football, crustaceans, or diesel mechanics. Most importantly, loose talk invited inquiries from police detectives and game wardens, outsiders whose interest in the routine illegalities of the waterfront was an annoying burden.

I brought a round of beer to a group near the pool table.

"I'm telling you," said a burly man with a scabbed nose, "the motherfucker is dead."

"What do you mean, dead?"

"I mean dead, with his head smashed in and green shit coming out the sides, dead."

"Horse shit. How you know that?"

"I just know, is how I know. Ol' Ray, you know Ray from San Leon? He's got a brother-in-law that was there when it happened. They were putting up a pole for this floodlight when the hoist broke. He wasn't looking, and it fell smack on top of him. Dead before he knew what hit him."

"Hell of a way to eat it."

"Well, there ain't no good ways, is there?"

"In the water, man. That's the way. When I die, I want 'em to bury my ass in the bay. That way one of you bastards can catch me and tear shit outta your rig."

"Shit. Ol' Jesse was lucky somebody didn't catch his ass. When he fell in the creek that night, I thought sure the tide would carry him out to Redfish."

"Didn't, though. Musta got tangled in some channel trash. Fucker popped up two slips away."

"It's hell waitin' for a guy to pop after he's drowned. Whole creek gets nervous, looking at the water all the time, waitin'."

"Especially the restaurants. They don't want no stiffs popping in front of the tourists during dinner."

"Remember when that Mexican popped over by the Jambalaya? Nobody even knew who the hell he was."

"Yeah. Damn tourists in the restaurant went nuts. Larson never gave away so many free meals in his life."

"The one that got me was that waitress gal from Adelia. Propeller musta got on her or somethin', she was so chewed up."

"Oh, yeah. That one used to go to school with my nephew. Nice girl, too. Wouldn't a said shit if she had a mouthful of it."

Everyone shook his head and reached for his beer.

"You know, there oughta be more drownin's, what with all them sailboats and motorboats zipping around out there. Ain't one of them assholes knows what the fuck he's doing."

Back at the bar, Donna was opening a beer for Vernon

Cutwell, a curly blonde with forearms twice as thick as his biceps. His Schlitz can, which he bent inadvertently as he took it, looked like a miniature in his fist. He swallowed a long drink and waited for Donna to initiate the waterfront greeting ritual.

"Well, Vern," she said, "how'd ya do today?"

He shifted his weight and looked away.

"Got me a few."

On the docks, how'd-ya-do and got-me-a-few went together like thanks and you're welcome. Anyone pressing for a better answer was rude. Those who volunteered more were judged dumb as a hammer.

I listened while Vernon told Donna the latest.

"You know ol' Tilton, the welder down at Pettigrew's? Told me this old boy come by when he heard Tilton was runnin' the VFW banquet. Called himself a free lance shrimp distributor."

Vernon took a sip from his damaged can.

"So the guy says, `Hey, I can get you a real good deal on a couple hunnerd pounds of tail.' So Tilton, he says, `Son, you ain't seen my wife. I already got a couple hunnerd pounds of tail back at the house.'"

"Now, Vernon," Donna laughed, "that ain't very nice."

"The hell it ain't. You ever seen his wife? Two hunnerd pounds is being, well, diplomatic about the thing."

Donna winked at me.

"So, Vern, she's pretty good size?"

He straightened his back for the put-away.

"Pretty good size! Hell, you could use her damn panty hose for a try net!"

Vernon's ears turned purple with pleasure. Donna brought out another beer and gave him a congratulatory stroke on the forearm. She ran a great bar.

It was clear that beer was a key ingredient of waterfront life, and the way a man used it meant a lot. How much he drank, how he drank it, the way he held his can—every detail told a story. Even the brew of choice made a difference. Eight of ten shrimpers preferred Schlitz, and everyone else drank Lone Star. No other brands seemed to exist. The marina did stock Bud for the occasional Houston dandy who stopped in for local color. But no man was taken seriously at Tina's with a red can in his hand.

Time passed pleasantly that afternoon, as it usually did in Tina's, and I found myself swept up in the fellowship of the place. Daisy, the evening barmaid, showed up a few minutes before three o'clock, which meant my first shift in the marina was drawing to a close. I paid for a Schlitz, drank it quickly, and replaced it with another. After a bumpy start, my first days on the water now seemed a rousing success, and I was emboldened to make my way out among the tables. Donna was my ticket to a deck hand's job, but this seemed an excellent way to make myself known among the captains of the fleet.

"Well," I said, sliding into an empty chair by the pool table. "How about that rain today? Looked a lot worse than it turned out, didn't it?"

Silence. The man beside me communicated wordlessly with the man across from him. Two other men at the table looked at their beer cans.

"Yeah," I said. "Petered out pretty quick."

One of the men glanced at me and then found something interesting on the back of his hand. His neighbor yawned as though I had never spoken. After about thirty excruciating seconds of this, I glanced back at the bar, where Daisy pretended she didn't notice. Donna had the look of a woman whose son was being strapped into an electric chair.

Finally I felt my legs move beneath me, and I seemed to levitate toward the register. Donna touched my hand and apologized for not stopping me in time.

"Let's get out of here," she said.

I followed her meekly to the parking lot, wondering if I would ever regain feeling in my upper body. Donna pointed to a faded green Falcon and told me to get in.

"Gotta pick up the little rascal," she said. "You and me can have us a talk on the way."

Donna pulled onto the asphalt and asked for my beer. Her mouth closed around it the way a kid's does when he imitates a fish.

"Don't let what happened in there bother you," she said softly. "They ain't no better than you, Sam, no matter what they think."

She started to hand back the Schlitz, but I waved it off. "I don't get it," I said. "I was just trying to be friendly, introduce myself around."

"I know, Sam. You meant well, but that just ain't the way things work down here. These men figure it ain't your place to go around talking to them."

"What a crock."

"You're right, Sam, pure dee shit. But there it is. Someday—before too long, I imagine—you're gonna understand. It's my fault for not warning you off."

"This is crazy. Here I am, a full-grown man—or I'm supposed to be, anyway. So why do I feel like a mortified goddamn child?"

Donna patted my knee and said, "Now, now, baby. Momma's here."

Without intending it, I gave her a look that made her pull her hand away.

"I'm sorry, Sam. I...I didn't know."

"Didn't know what?" I felt a sudden, alarming chill. "What are you talking about?"

"Well...you know..." She shifted in her seat, trying not to confront me directly. "Sam...you know, I lost my mother, too...when I was young."

"But, how could you possibly—"

"How old were you, Sam?"

"Six," I said. My voice began to thicken, but not in grief for my mother, who had been dead so many years. Rather I was stunned because Donna had discerned it. Was it genius on her part, or utter transparency on mine?

"It must have been hard, Sam. That's awful young to lose a mother."

"Not so bad. Well, it was sad, of course. But it was harder for Dad than for me. I was so young that after awhile, being without her was all I ever really knew."

"You can say that, but that don't make it easy." Donna forced the beer back into my hand. "But don't you worry about nothing, now. Just stick close to me, and you're gonna be fine. I promise."

She turned into a trailer court and waved at Jaquita, who from that distance appeared to have a golf ball attached to her big toe.

"Poor thing," Donna said. "She's got more trouble with corns and bunions than anybody you ever heard of. She needs to stop wearing them pointy-ass shoes."

Sharlene popped up from a circle of children and ran for the car, clasping a bouquet of weeds. Her mouth was red with Kool-Aid.

"How was your afternoon?" Donna said, opening her door. Sharlene hopped onto the seat between us and indicated it had been an absolute two.

"Well, don't I get some sugar?"

Sharlene shook her head in mock disgust and offered her bouquet to me.

"Two," I said. "Two you very much."

"She's really shining up to you, Sam. Sharlene's always been a good judge of men." She reached down and squeezed the girl's tanned little leg. "Unlike old Donna here. Right, rascal?"

"Two!"

Sharlene crawled into my lap as we drove away and soon was letting the wind play with her hand outside the window. The scent of her hair, shampooed with the same bottle as Donna's, brought back the afternoon in a rush. I saw again the thin white scar against the redness of Donna's face, felt the strength of her fingers pressing my hands to her breasts. For a brief moment, Donna had seemed to want me. And I knew that I—despite her age, despite my rawness, despite everything—had wanted her.

Eventually Donna pulled up to Tina's again, and I began reliving the spectacular gaffe with which I'd ended the day. I wondered aloud whether I had ruined my chances for a deckhand's job.

"Don't worry," Donna said brightly. "You leave that to me. Just remember: From now on, let me do the talking."

"Like the lamb led to slaughter, I shall open not my mouth."

Donna and Sharlene exchanged puzzled looks.

"Looks like we got us a live one, kiddo. What do you think?

"Two!"

"You got that right."

I climbed out of the car and stood beneath Tina's left breast. Sharlene stuck out her tongue as they backed out and then threw kisses until the car pulled away. I am usually slow to warm to children, but Sharlene was something else again. It was impossible not to be swept up in the wry charm that animated her. And her zest for living seemed the highest possible endorsement of Donna.

Yet back in my room upstairs, I came upon something peculiar. I'd left the bed unmade that morning with the pillow pinned between the mattress and the wall. The sheets were still ruffled now, but in a different way, and the pillow was patted flat at the head of the bed.

I wondered if Donna, wherever she was, would awaken with a start that night, her gray eyes focusing vainly in the dark.

*   *   *

After a quick shower that evening I went downstairs and found Bunny struggling with the uneven shells on the parking lot. She was on her way to a pickup truck driven by a man whose shoulders seemed to fill the cab. They took no notice of one another when Bunny climbed aboard. She dug for something in her purse while he crushed a beer can with one hand. But when she caught sight of me on the dock, the dynamics in the cab immediately changed.

Bunny pulled her man's giant arm from the gearshift, climbed to her knees and started chewing his ear. He eventually found the shifter again, and she stole a quick glance at me as the truck pulled away. The last thing I saw was the Hogner ass, pantied and cocked up to the sky, pressed against the window like a white hippopotamus.

It was definitely time for a beer.

I spent the evening wandering from bar to bar, an explorer in the catacombs, trying to learn what I could about my uncharted new life. Vietnamese shrimpers—and the firestorms that met them on the Gulf coast—were more than a year away in 1974. In the self-imposed social quarantine of the docks, there was evidence that the last two digits of the year had somehow been transposed.

Men still cut their hair like Harry Truman and rolled cigarette packs into their shirt sleeves. Women, with Donna a pleasant exception, sculpted their hair into bee hives and wore pointed brassieres. Even television didn't exist for the grizzled souls on the waterfront. Day and night, it was a world so insular that Richard Nixon's last presidential gasps passed almost unnoticed.

By sundown I had seen and drunk quite enough for one evening. I was watching the moon from my bed when someone knocked downstairs. What I saw when I opened the door gave me a start: Knuckles Dupree in the dark, with his mouth wide open.

"Hello, evrabody! Hello there, one and all."

I leaned heavily against the stair rail.

"Looks like you had ya a coupla cool ones," he said. "Maybe the last one got to ya some."

"Not at all," I said, still unsure about what to make of this. "It was me against six cans, and I was the only one left standing."

Knuckles put his giant hands on his head and roared. He'd apparently drained a few cans himself.

"Donna told me you're practical running this place already."

"Well, I'm not on a boat yet, but I've got a job and a room until I do. I want to thank you again for helping me out yesterday."

"Well, dat's no problem. I expect you'll find something directly."

"Yeah, if there's a skipper dumb enough to hire a kid with baby-butt hands."

Knuckles looked puzzled. He'd heard that somewhere before.

"You'll do fine," he said. "If you been to college, maybe it won't take too long to learn your way around a boat."

His face brightened. "That reminds me how come I'm here. I got a little trouble with my winch, and it takes two peoples to fix it. Donna told me you're all interested in boats and all. She said if I came by you might want to give me a hand."

I leaped into step behind him and almost snapped an ankle on the shells, which were deceptively contourless in the dark. By the time we reached the smoother ground beside Bunny's office, I realized I had held my breath all the way. I was out of wind and drunker than ever.

"Where," I gasped, "where is the boat?"

"We practical on it now," Knuckles said. "It's up there, next to the pear fo."

Two hundred yards ahead of us was the blinking neon sign advertising the Pier Four restaurant. When we reached it the surrounding air was bursting with a brutal stink. The dumpster beside the building was filled with fish heads, crabs, shrimp shells and other varieties of wet garbage—all of it baked to a rancid freshness through the afternoon. And there was Knuckles' boat, not fifteen feet away.

"Jesus, how can you stand it?" I said, spitting into the creek.

"Stand what?"

Knuckles stepped quickly onto the catwalk alongside his boat. I saw the six-inch plank I would have to negotiate and wished I had come across Knuckles seventy-two ounces earlier. I trusted myself on the pier for only a few steps and then hopped aboard.

The Foxy Lady was a rusty bucket that looked as if it hadn't been cleaned in thirty years. But like its skipper's face, it was a rich mosaic of experience, the real thing, the stuff I'd come here for. I drank up the squeaks and smells and thought of the storms it must have weathered, the tons of fish it must have brought back to shore.

Knuckles was on the stern, arranging some folds of net. He told me to get his crowbar from under the bunk.

"Light's busted in the cabin," he said. "You'll have to use that flashlight by the switch."

I was surprised Knuckles had wandered from his cabin with the door unlocked. But the stench inside explained why the boat was secure from burglars—and why Knuckles didn't notice the dumpster on shore.

The flashlight beam found trash everywhere, including smashed beer cans that were beginning to rust. The bunk was nothing but a bare mattress splotched with oil and other stains that were beyond identification. I couldn't see a crowbar, so I sank to my knees and aimed the flashlight under the bunk. Nothing was there but filthy rags and clothes, and I pushed some away to aim the beam farther back. I saw a coil of rope in the corner—It moved. A head rose from the coil, and two black eyes glinted in the beam. Snake. The eyes contracted and went yellow. It drew back its head and hissed. I was kneeling in the dark with a flashlight in my hand, staring down an angry snake.

I hit my head on the bunk trying to get free and landed heavily on the floor. The flashlight rolled away. Something was on my leg—God, get it off. I grabbed a shelf and heard a crash of beer cans, then stumbled to the door and caught something in my stomach. Forget that, idiot, get away. The door slammed into the wall. I was out.

Knuckles was lying on the net with his knees drawn up to his stomach, almost epileptic with laughter.

"Trouble?" he gasped. "Sounded like a fistfight in there."

I saw white.

"Are you fucking crazy? You want to get somebody killed? I ought to rip your goddamn throat out."

Only when I imagined myself reaching toward his cruelly etched face did I realize what I'd said.

"Uh-oh." Knuckles began to find his breath. "I guess you met ol' Joe. He general stays under the bunk. Me and him, we been partners a long time."

I grabbed a rigging bar and rested my forehead against it. I could feel my heart pounding everywhere, in my hands, in my ears—even in my balls, which were drawn up into me like spooked hermit crabs.

"Don't let Joe bother ya." It was a cheerful woman's voice on shore. Donna's voice. "He's a pussycat, Sam. Just a bow constrictor, is all. Ain't a drop of poison in him."

"You," I said. "You put him up to this."

Donna reached down in the darkness and pulled a sleepy Sharlene onto her hip. "Well, maybe we did do a little instigatin'."

"Hope you ain't mad," Knuckles said. "I only show Joe to my friends."

I looked at his craggy face and his twitching stump of a tongue, and I knew he meant it. Knuckles didn't have what it took to be insincere. I smeared my face with a forearm and said no, I wasn't mad.

"Just surprised is all. Soon as I clean the shit out of my pants I'll help you with the winch—but you get the crowbar."

Donna laughed. "Nothin' wrong with no winch, Sam."

I began to notice the breeze again, and it felt good against my face.

"Guess I've had enough excitement for one night," I said. "Tell Joe it was nice to meet him."

"Will do," Knuckles said, adjusting a clump of net under his head. That was where he would spend the night.

I hopped onto the plank and strolled toward Donna with a new confidence. I had actually chewed out Knuckles Dupree and survived. Ah, the sweet, triumphant thrill of it all.

Donna looped her free arm through mine, and we walked out toward the pungent smell of tar patches on the road. Cars were crossing the metal grate of the bridge, and the sky was brighter than ever with stars. Back at the marina, Donna nestled Sharlene onto a blanket on the front seat and then turned toward me. We listened to the wind and the tide and simply looked at one another—she deciphering every emotion within me, I hoping she was bold enough to act on what she saw.

Finally she raised a single finger to her lips, moistened it, then pressed it gently against mine. I watched, helpless, as she stepped to her car and drove away without a word.

When she was gone I decided to spend a few quiet minutes on the patio before closing my eyes on the day. The neon lights across the creek glittered on the water like snow crystals. I traced the line of channel beacons out into the bay and for a brief moment, a moment lost when Conway Twitty took to the jukebox, I imagined I had seen into the very heart and soul of this place.

Four

Wednesday reveille was a lot easier on the heart than Tuesday's, but the morning brought troubling new mysteries. Reaching for the electric razor, I kicked something near the dresser. There, peeking up from the dust, was a shiny brown wallet.

It seemed a pleasant enough way to start the day—at best I was rich, and at worst I could spend the morning grazing through someone's secrets. The highest hope was quickly dashed: only two tens and a single. I fumbled through the pockets and pulled out a driver's license—Donna's license. I had hit the jackpot after all.

The wallet was the kind of crudity found in Cub Scout dens and curios shops—thin strips of leather joined by plastic laces, with Western scenes etched into the hide. I held it up to see how much of her life Donna carried with her. Not very much, it turned out—no bulging pockets, no photo sleeves. All she had was a gasoline credit card, some credit slips, and the license. Not one creased family portrait, no secret phone numbers, not a juicy tidbit in the lot. There was nothing left but to stretch out in bed and linger over the license awhile.

Had the eyes in the picture not been taking such careful measure of the camera, I might have been persuaded it was someone else. The Donna here was younger and heavier, with teased hair and—biggest shock of all—the trace of a sneer. Her lips were almost closed, but they couldn't hide teeth that were slightly large for her mouth.

Donna Bedicek. I hadn't known her last name, but it fit the shadows in the photograph. The strength in her face owed much to a Czech bone structure which gave her a farmer's jaw and a thin, angular nose. Donna was fresh from the beauty parlor, but the bubble that engulfed her head was far less flattering than her pony tail. Yet her eyes were just as urgent, just as hungry, as the ones I had seen.

It occurs to me now, these many years later, how seldom I saw anything like abstraction in Donna's pale eyes. Always, always, even when she laughed, her face was filled with the present, the physical here and now. I can't even remember how she looked when she blinked, if her alertness ever allowed that luxury.

Sitting alone in my room with Donna's remarkable face was a treat, yet the longer I looked at her, the more impenetrable she became. *You don't know about people like me.* I looked for clues in the set of her mouth, her suspicion of the photographer, the laugh lines that here looked vaguely like a wince.

She was right—I didn't know, and I wasn't even close. The most startling proof was in her birth date. Donna Bedicek, my toothless, wrinkled, battered aunt of a friend, was thirty-three years old.

*   *   *

I turned to the matter of how Donna's wallet had found its way upstairs. My hunch about the altered bed linens now seemed confirmed, and Leo Sanchez' nervous departure from the marina made new sense. He had seemed unnaturally pleased to see me behind the bar—and he even mentioned that Donna would now have chances to get away during the day.

But there were other, more savory, possibilities. Donna might have dropped her wallet weeks before while carrying supplies from the attic. She might have taken a nap after work when the room was still vacant. Maybe I had imagined the altered linens, and it was possible that Leo had gone straight to his car.

I occurred to me to flip through the credit receipts. Bingo. Donna had charged gas on Monday, her day off. She could only have dropped the wallet here when I was downstairs Tuesday. Yes, she had come in the room without asking or telling me about it.

I checked the drawers. Everything was in place. It was clearer than ever that I didn't know Donna, but I doubted she was a thief. She must have been here with Leo—and she must have had a reason to take her wallet out during their visit. I began to feel Bunny Hogner's fingers on my cheek again. *Watch out for that Donna.*

Should I confront her with the wallet and demand an explanation? Throw it away and forget it? Return it to the floor as if I'd never found it? Surely Donna would discover the loss soon—if she hadn't already—and trace her steps back to my room. I had to decide before I saw her again.

This wasn't worth a hostile confrontation, but she'd been so secretive with me I couldn't let it pass. I found some paper and wrote, "If you want to come into my room, all you have to do is ask." Then I slipped the sheet conspicuously behind the money and dropped the wallet back to the floor.

By six thirty that morning I was finished with the outside chores and perched next to Knuckles at the bar. I looked for hints of apprehension in Donna, but she was bathed once again in her cheerful morning glow. She either didn't know about the wallet, or she was skilled enough to hide it.

"You know," she said, "I'm afraid that one of these days Knucks is gonna get killed over that Joe stunt."

Knuckles grinned mischievously. He was wearing the same clothes he'd met me in—the same clothes that would last him most of the summer.

"Why come that is?" he said.

"You might not have noticed, my friend, but there's people in this world who don't love snakes as much as you do."

"That may be. But I personal think it's a shame, in my opinion. Peoples could learn a lot from snakes."

Donna winked at me and propped her chin on her forearms.

"You take your food," Knuckles began. "A man don't need much food to get by on, whether he's a person or a snake. Old Joe, he gets him a rat on the boat every now and then, and he's happy as he can be. Peoples eat way too much, and that's why come they's all so unhappy.

"You take me. I come in here every day at six. I take coffee for an hour for my vitamins. Then all I need is my beer the rest of the day."

"Wait a minute," I said. "How can you survive without solid food?"

"Oh, I'll eat me a hot dog fo' I go to bed some days, if my stomach's gone sour. Usual don't need it, though. You think about a beer now. It's got yeast in there, grain, some salt, maybe a little sugar. It's flat-out full of groceries. I'm fifty-nine year old, and it's kept me going as long as I remember."

I stifled the urge to ask how far back the regimen let him recall. Donna assured him he didn't look a day over eighty-five.

Knuckles started filing his cigarette ash to a point on the bar. "You know," he said suddenly, "I didn't always used to be a fool old man. They was a time when peoples used to say I favored John Wayne."

That was surprising at first, but I began to see the similarities. He certainly had the squint.

"It's the sun that takes it out of ya, makes your face old."

"'Least you got your teeth," Donna said. "You lose them things, and the years go right along with 'em."

At that instant I felt the rush a thief must get when he's jimmied a door.

"It's not so bad," I said. "I'll prove it, Donna. I'll bet I can guess your age."

"Oh, you can? That'll be the day."

"If you're so sure, put a dollar on it."

She grinned at Knuckles. "Fair enough. This'll be easy money."

"First thing," I said, "let me see your hands."

Her fingers were slender, but the skin was tough and crusted. One of her fingernails had been blackened in an accident.

"Now, with your stronger hand, grab my thumb and squeeze as hard as you can."

She chewed her tongue while she did it.

"Donna, you are thirty-three years old."

Her lips went slack, and she pulled away. Knuckles dropped a giant hand on my shoulder.

"Better get out your money, boy. I coulda done better with one eye closed."

"Well," I said, "am I in the ballpark?"

Donna grinned uncomfortably and said, "Looks like I owe somebody a dollar."

Knuckles looked at me with his mouth open. Donna reached for her purse and fumbled for the wallet I knew was on the floor above us. She looked annoyed, then puzzled.

"Shit," she muttered, straining to remember where she'd seen it last. When she looked at me again it came to her.

"Musta left my wallet in the car," she said calmly. "You watch the bar, okay? I hope I haven't lost it."

She took her purse and was gone less than a minute. She came back in looking stricken.

"Any luck?"

She shrugged without answering and pushed her purse back under the register. Later that morning I slipped upstairs, and the wallet was gone. Donna didn't say a word when I came back, but the set of her lips showed she knew where I had been.

I never had the nerve to ask for my dollar, but I realize now the incident cost me so much more. That was the moment when all the illusions I needed in my life began to fade away.

Five

Donna and I were so polite to one another the rest of the morning that I soon began hating myself for what I'd done. Her sin, after all, had been a small one, and she had done so much to welcome me to the waterfront. The more I thought about it, the more my prank seemed cruel. Still, there were questions that wouldn't go away.

Had I discovered a secret romance between Leo and his favorite barmaid? Or was it one of many conquests for the toothless siren? Maybe a waterfront sugar daddy and his babe—or was it simple commerce? Every scenario cast a different light on the shapely belle behind the bar. Did she watch herself when she rested her chin so innocently on her forearms? Did she really care what the Schlitz-on-a-stool boys had to say?

One thing was certain: I knew something that Donna didn't want me to know, and it placed her in a kind of jeopardy. I tried to think of some way to make a fresh start, but every plan smelled false. It fell to Leo Sanchez to end the stalemate.

I was leveling the pool table when he bounced in just before noon, once again all smiles and good cheer. He gave me a jaunty wave and winked at Donna while she brought out his cup and can. But when she sat at the table and started whispering the new developments, it didn't take long for his smile to disappear. They spoke quietly, and it was clear they were arguing about what to do. Leo looked away every time I glanced at them. Finally Donna pushed back her chair and shuffled toward the pool table, her eyes fixed on the felt.

"You said I should ask before I go in your room."

There was a pathetic silence.

"Well, I'm asking."

My stomach began to tighten. Donna, who had seemed the very essence of proud self-possession, could not lift her eyes from the table. I looked at Leo, sitting like a Bhudda with his Schlitz can and his plastic cup and his fat yellow tongue licking foam from his lips. And I said sure, Donna, it's okay, and I imagined myself taking a pool cue from the rack and bashing it right across his satisfied face.

*   *   *

When Donna and Leo were upstairs, Bunny Hogner's voice came back again and again: *Watch out for that Donna.* But Leo had been the one staring blandly out the window while Donna came to me with her head bowed. It was easy to see who the victim was.

Or was it? Donna was the one with the stark eyes, the one who had lied so easily about breaking into my room. Had she offered up her dignity for her man or his money? I wasn't sure I wanted to find out.

The marina was empty when Donna came down, alone. She poured a cup of coffee and then looked out at the creek.

"You've got to promise me something," she said. "Please don't tell Bunny what you know, or I'm dead."

I was disappointed that this was the first thing she'd chosen to say.

"Go ahead, Sam." She turned to confront me. "Let me hear from you. Don't just sit there and stare."

I groped for something profound and then suddenly lost patience.

"I don't know, Donna. Guys like me, we don't understand."

I regretted saying it before I was even finished. Bringing up yesterday's hedge about her teeth was vicious now—vicious enough to take her off the defensive.

"You don't have the right to butt into my life, you know."

"You're right, but I don't recall breaking into your room."

She cut me off.

"Okay, you're so interested in my goddamn teeth, I'll tell you. You're gonna be sorry you ever asked."

"That's not the point."

"I used to be hooked up with a guy, this creep, who liked what I could do for him without my dentures in."

I swallowed sickly and said, "I don't think I—"

"He really liked it, see? Liked it so much that one night when he was drunk, he took my teeth away. Said I didn't need 'em to please him. Said he wouldn't have to share me with nobody else if I didn't have no teeth.

"So he took 'em outside, out behind his house, and he blew 'em up with his shotgun."

She threw her coffee in the trash and glared at me.

"I finally got clear of him. But I ain't had a tooth in my head for months, and I ain't gonna have until I can pay the clinic for another set. And God knows when I'm gonna do that.

"There. Now you know all about me and my goddamn teeth."

Trying to defend myself was useless. She wouldn't hear it, and I didn't have the wind for it anyway. I was a peeping Tom caught at the window.

"So, you gonna tell Bunny or not?"

The question gave me a chance to recover.

"What do you think?"

The worry rinsed slowly from her face, and Donna edged toward me.

"I'm sorry, Sam. You don't deserve that. It's just...well, there's a lot—"

"Forget it. There's nothing for me to tell."

She took my hand with both of hers and raised it to her cheek.

"This is twice, now, that you've saved my life," she whispered. "No matter what happens, I'm always going to remember that."

*   *   *

And so began the illicit little conspiracy at the strange place called Tina's Marina. It certainly seemed a friendly and harmless routine. Leo appeared almost every day at eleven. (Donna knew a day in advance when he wouldn't.) He sat at the same window table, drank one beer from a cup, and pretended to ignore Donna as she drifted away. Moments later he would follow, and then she'd shuffle back, her purse over a shoulder, a quick half hour later.

Not many days passed before Leo was his animated self again. He even started leaving an occasional gift on my dresser. Maybe a paperback, or a magazine, or a half-pint of bourbon. I responded by leaving the room in perfect shape every morning. For the first time in my life I regularly made my bed, and I always found it made when I came back. There was a whole lotta shakin' goin' on behind Tina's handsome breasts, and I would have relished a chance to do some shaking myself. But at least I got a kinky little charge out my part in the arrangement.

Meanwhile my friendship with Donna blossomed like bluebonnets in March. She took genuine pleasure from enlightening me about the ways of the docks, and she seemed to regard my muddled insecurities with a sweet, maternal concern.

"The waterfront could use a lot more like you," she said more than once. "But you've got to watch out that it don't eat you alive."

The irony was that Donna herself was among its most wounded victims. The fetishist who destroyed her dentures happened also to be Bunny Hogner's boyfriend at the time. Rodney Gene kept Bunny from firing her in retaliation, but he made it clear that Donna would not be forgiven for job-related indiscretions. Her daily tumbles in the attic with Leo certainly qualified. And that meant Donna's fate rested in the pink hands of a college kid she had just met—and was only a blown secret away from resting in Bunny's.

An obvious question was why Donna risked so much to be with Leo. It was a question I never asked her, not so much because it was none of my business, but because I feared the answer. Donna was counting on me, and I was utterly taken with her. We each had reasons to see the other with forgiving eyes.

Without Donna as my entree, most of the mumbling shrimpers and dock hounds would have been strangers to me forever. She went out of her way to introduce me, and on the delicate occasions when it was appropriate, to draw me into their conversations. I can't remember how many times Donna saved me from myself.

One afternoon in the marina, an oyster shucker and a Borneo dock hand were ruminating about the decline of Western civilization. The shucker advanced the theory that effeminate men were at the core of the crisis.

"Pussies," he said. "The pussies and the peaceniks have took over the show. Take that goddamn McGovern idiot. I still can't believe they never threw that bastard in jail. All he wanted to do was give everything to the commies, and there he was, running for president. No wonder this country is going to hell."

"Excuse me," I chirped. "Now you're talking about my hero. George S. McGovern happens to be a great man."

"What'd he say?" The shucker was astonished.

"Just him trying to be funny," Donna said. I started to object, but she shot me such a look I thought I heard a Doberman bark. After a discreet interval Donna motioned me over to the pool table.

"Listen up for your own good," she whispered. "It's your right to like whoever you want. But you don't have to admit something like that in public."

My favorite times with Donna were the mid-day lulls after

Leo had gone. Our chores were usually finished by then, and the shrimpers hadn't yet returned from the bay. Donna and I would stand at the bar with the newspaper spread out between us, turning the pages slowly and clucking at the latest contortions of the human race. We were the only two people on the waterfront with the slightest interest in the printed word, and it was our habit to fold the paper quickly when we heard steps near the doors. But often as not we had the bar to ourselves, and always there was the bright vista spread out before us.

Watching a bay's infinite driftage can loosen deep adhesions in the soul. Donna soon knew everything about me, vowing to keep my career crisis to herself. And on one lazy afternoon, my Earth Mother of the Docks set aside her enduring caution and disclosed from whence she came.

*   *   *

Donna Alice Bedicek was born one year to the day before Pearl Harbor, in a farm house near Jewett in East Texas. Her parents were an unlikely couple—he would be too old for war, and she was too young to vote.

"Daddy met Momma on a farm in Arkansas," she told me. "She was there with her family, and he was a hired hand. Daddy was a shy man, so shy he'd been a bachelor all his life. He was almost fifty when he found her.

"But I guess it was really her that found him. My Momma had her ways. She was pretty and she was antsy—Momma used to say that from the day she could walk she was about half-crazy to walk off that farm. Well, she got away, all right. She was a few days shy of fifteen when they ran off together. Daddy was so bashful, especially around women, that I'm sure Momma had to pretty much lead him by the hand, even though she was just a baby herself. She must have figured Daddy was her best chance to get clear of the barnyard and see the world.

"They wound up having me in no time. We never stayed

in one place long. Must have lived in a hundred towns when I was growing up. Texas, Arkansas, Oklahoma, Louisiana. Daddy was raised on a farm in Missouri, but he could do a little bit of everything—farming, carpentry, cowboyin', plumbing. He was even a good electrician. He'd been pretty much of a drifter all his life before he met Momma, and he wasn't anxious to change. And she didn't want him to, neither. She was wild, and she liked it best when they were on the move. It was when they stayed someplace too long that things used to go sour."

Donna shook her head suddenly when she realized how much of herself she was giving away. "I haven't talked about my Momma in years." She pointed at me with both hands. "But you. You gotta know everything about everything."

"Just the facts, ma'am. You've already got the goods on me."

"All right, but don't go blabbing this stuff all over the docks."

I had to smile at that. No one would have paid attention to me if I'd tried.

"Anyway, she was wilder than wild, my Momma. Probably a little insane, if you want to know the truth. She used to work on Daddy, you know, work on his mind. Make fun of him because he was awkward, try to make him jealous. I imagine she realized pretty quick after she left home that Daddy couldn't bring her the world on a plate after all. I think she decided to make him pay for that. But it wasn't like he broke any promises. She was the one with the big ideas.

"Every time we'd come to a town someplace, Daddy would find him a job, and pretty soon you'd hear Momma complaining about how boring it all was. How she always wanted to see Paris and Rome and every place else, and how they were never gonna make it the way they were going. She'd get to sulking, and she'd give Daddy the needle when he came home, griping about how he never wanted to go out and have any fun. Daddy was such a sweet old fool, he just put up with it."

I asked if they were still married.

"Both of 'em dead," she said quickly. "Daddy had more than thirty years on Momma, but she was the first to go."

She shook her head and studied something across the creek.

"I remember one time we were at a picnic someplace—I was too young to know where. It was some kind of company deal, put on by the mill my daddy was working at. All the men were there with their wives and their kids—it was just Momma and Daddy and me then.

"I don't know whether they had beer, or Momma was sneakin' from a flask, but she wound up getting pretty drunk by the middle of the day. I remember her talking real loud and laughing a lot, teasin' on Daddy and all. He was embarrassed as he could be, and he kept trying to hush her. Well, naturally, it didn't do no good.

"The more he tried to calm her down, the rowdier she got. Before long she had a bunch of the men playin' up to her— Momma always was a flashy one with the fellas—and she started playin' right back to them. They were joking and she was giggling and eventually they all started talking about going for a swim in this little pond out there.

"Momma wound up being the first one to jump in, cotton dress and all. She was splashing and making such a racket that all the other women started noticing what was going on, and that was the end of the swimming right there. Only thing was, Momma was still in the pond, and pretty soon everybody was gathered around looking. Daddy went in—I remember he still had his good shoes on—and tried to help her get back. Only she got mad and started cussing him out. The water musta took the edge off her drunk.

"Anyway, she finally came out of the pond, and the dress was just glued to her body. It was a light color, and you could see right through it. I was standing next to this boy, and he blurted out what everybody was thinking: `She ain't got no underwear on!' Momma heard it, and that made her madder than ever. `So what if I ain't?' she says. And then she picked her dress all the way up in front and started wringing it out. People scattered like she'd thrown a hand grenade."

Donna laughed softly to herself.

"That was my mother, right there. Just did what she wanted when she wanted to, and to hell with whoever didn't like it—including Daddy. I'm sure he had to quit the mill after that one. But Momma, she wouldn't have given a damn."

"She sounds like something else," I said. "But it must have been tough for her, too. She had you so soon...and she must have been quite young when she died."

"I was ten. My little sister, Jamie, she was six. To this day, she still blames Daddy for it. But if you ask me, Momma was the one that killed Daddy."

Donna grew quiet. I asked what she meant.

"It goes back to that other business. You know, that stuff about Momma always making Daddy suffer for what he couldn't give her. Eventually she got to where she started carrying on with other men, goin' to bars by herself when Daddy was at work—and sometimes even when he was home. Usually she'd leave me and my sister alone at the house. But once in a while she'd take us with her.

"I was a little girl, but it wasn't no mystery to me what was going on. I remember one time we were at this fella's house, and Momma told us to go play out in the backyard. Well, she and this fella were upstairs in the bedroom, and since it was summertime the window was wide open. They weren't being very bashful about things, and we could hear everything that was going on up there.

"I remember my sister—she was about five—started going all wild. `Momma's crying,' she says. `That man's hurting her! We gotta make him stop!'

"I told her there wasn't nobody hurtin' nobody, so just leave it alone. But Jamie kept on yelling and screaming so much that Momma finally stuck her head out and told her to cool off. So then my little sister, she says, `Donna, how come Momma's wearing that man's shirt?'"

Donna managed a smile, then leaned forward suddenly.

"She wasn't bad, my Momma. Ignorant, I guess. Ignorant the way a spoiled baby's ignorant. She couldn't take care of herself, so she stayed with Daddy. But she was smart enough to know she'd never get what she wanted. Never in a million years. Even after everything she did to Daddy, I could never hate her all out, because she had to live with that."

As Donna walked our coffee cups to the bar for refills, it occurred to me that she was older then than her mother had been at the picnic, or in the stranger's house—or on her deathbed. I looked at the front door and prayed there were no customers within miles of it.

"Your mother," I said. "If you were ten when she died, she must have been, what, just twenty-five?"

Donna looked out toward the bay.

"Sounds right," she finally said. "You know, everything in all our lives—Daddy's, Momma's, Jamie's, mine—it all either started or finished on that one single day, when Momma passed. How about you, Sam? Ever had a day like that, a day when everything changes?"

"No, but that's probably the kind of day I need."

"You say that, but you don't mean it. You should hope it never happens."

She shuffled back to the table, and her gray eyes suddenly brightened.

"Matter of fact, we were living in your town, Fort Worth, in those days. Daddy was working real hard in some factory or other—gone all the time. One night he came home all wore out and Momma started in on him. How come he's never home? What's she supposed to do with herself all day and all night? How would he like it if she just took off without him for a change?

"But this time Daddy took it different. Instead of sitting there quiet the way he always did, he sorta snapped. He grabbed her by the hair and pulled her to the front door. `You wanna go,' he says, `then this is the way out. But if you go, this time you're gonna stay gone.'

"When he let her go, Momma acted real calm. She straightened her hair, got her purse and walked out. And that was the last time I ever saw her."

"What happened?"

"Don't know exactly. All I know for sure is, there was a bunch of unpleasantness that night on Jacksboro Highway. Something about a bunch of men from a beer joint taking out after her, and her getting killed. Daddy never would tell us what really happened.

"Anyway, nothing was the same after that. Daddy was never right again, it tore him up so. He got to be a pretty good drinker himself, and he died of a stroke when I was sixteen. I'll always say it was Momma that killed him."

She fixed her eyes on me and smiled wearily.

"I never was the same, neither," she said. I grew up in one night. I had to keep the house, take care of my little sister, help Daddy when he was too drunk to get out of his chair. And my little sister, it made her hate him. She said it was Daddy who killed Momma by making her go."

I tried to imagine a smooth-faced Donna of sixteen. And I wondered if that was the year her eyes found their fire.

"My mother's mother was still living then, and she took us back on her farm in Arkansas. Me and her never did get along. She blamed Daddy, just like Jamie did, and she kept turning my sister against him. It didn't take me long to see why my Momma wanted off that place. I left about three months after I got there. Been on my own ever since."

Donna became vague about events after the farm. High school was an impossibility, and there was a long procession of jobs in bars, cafes, washaterias. Then she drifted to a fish house on the bay—and even had a brief stint on a shrimp boat. Two summers before I met her, Donna opened a small bar of her own on the Maxwell side. It was swept away in a storm the following spring. She had been at Tina's just over a year.

I have thought often of her parents' marriage, if indeed there had been a ceremony. It was a volatile union of youth and experience, patience and promiscuity—and the same was true of its firstborn. Donna had her mother's Ozark drawl and her father's flat Missouri dipthongs, the body of a young woman and the face of an old one. Resting her chin on her forearms was a habit she might have learned from her gentle father. The trysts in the attic seemed a legacy of his spouse.

If, as Donna said, her life began at ten when her mother died, then she and I were born at about the same time in the same town near the same row of chicken-wire beer joints. Since then we had taken such different paths, and it shamed me to think that I had considered mine arduous. But after all that had happened we were here now, adrift together in the same waterfront bar.

"What about Sharlene?" I said. "When did she come into the fray?"

Donna fidgeted with her coffee cup before she answered.

"That was about a year ago. Her momma had been one of my barmaids, and that's how I got roped into the deal. Not that I mind, though. Sharlene's about the best thing I got going."

I remembered what Donna had said about her own mother, that she was someone to be pitied and not reviled. Pregnant at fifteen with the scents of the backwoods still in her hair, she'd been bright enough to know what she wanted and quick enough to know she'd never get it.

I wondered if that was the lesson the bay ultimately had in store for me. And I asked Donna what it was that she wanted from her life.

"Nothing," she said, with a surprising sharpness. "I learned to spare myself that grief a long time ago. I saw what hopes and dreams did to Momma."

I started to answer, but she held up her hand.

"Sam, I know what I'm talking about. Plans just make you unhappy with what you've got. They mess with your mind, make you do things you got no business doing. There's enough trouble in the world without you making more of it inside yourself.

"So, since you're asking, take it from somebody who

knows: If you want to be happy in this world, the best thing is to wipe every bit of trouble from your mind."

For a mixed-up sad sack on the run from the world and himself, no words could have been as comforting—or as dangerous—as those.

Six

One morning during my ritual baptism of the dock, I heard the telephone ring behind the bar. Moments later Donna wandered outside to share the sunrise. Leo, she said, wasn't going to make it that day.

"Nothing wrong, I hope."

"Naw," she sighed, "just something he's got to take care of in Galveston. Looks like I've got a lunch hour to kill."

I felt a tingle. Many times in my imagination I had taken Leo's place in the attic, easing Donna gently from her clothes and leaning back on the mattress as her hips strained above me...

Donna rested her forearms on a piling and lost herself in the pink mural to the east. The breeze played with her pony tail and pressed her T-shirt tight against her skin. She shivered just perceptibly as I looked, and her nipples stirred to life. She was indeed a beautiful woman—but for the temporary misfortune of her mouth, a stunning one. Knowing her real age made her appear younger, and my daily familiarity with her had the effect of obscuring her only real flaw.

In time everyone loses sight of his best friend's walleye or the burn scars on his cousin's back. There is so much in a human companion to distract the attention. But with Donna there was something else at work. As we became closer, her mouth seemed less a shortcoming than a tender symbol of vulnerability.

Standing beside her that morning, knowing that Leo wouldn't have her on my bed, I began to admit how much I wanted Donna, wanted to lose myself inside her, to bathe forever in her warm, consoling glow. And yes, I would admit this, too: I wanted that which had moved another man to blow her dentures into a thousand irretrievable bits.

Eventually she turned toward me, and her face showed once again she had taken her magical step beyond empathy.

"It would be nice, Sam, but we'd better not. We don't want to mess up a good thing, do we?"

"Sure do," I blurted, almost giddy with relief for having done it.

Donna reached up for my cheek, as if to reproach herself with how smooth and young it was. Then she looked beyond me to the bay.

"Sam, you haven't seen me more than five minutes away from this place. You don't know nothing about what I really am, about the way I live—"

"I know enough."

She smiled wanly and let her hand fall to my chest. I was emboldened to trace the outline of her breast, and when she didn't stop me I drew close.

"This is a mistake," she said.

"No, Donna, it's not."

"I've been worried about this since the day you showed up."

"I know this woman who says if you want to be happy in this world, the best thing is to wipe every bit of trouble from your mind."

She smiled again and wound her arms around me. "Just...just don't kiss me," she said. But I kissed her forehead and her ear and the scar on her cheek, and then I found her lips, as soft as new lace, and thought I would faint when she let me inside them.

She pulled away to look at me, her face an indescribable mixture of sadness and joy. Then she reached for my hand.

"We're both going to regret this," she sighed. "But come

on—Knuckles is just going to have to wait awhile for his vitamins."

*   *   *

For the rest of the morning the sun was bright, the air was
busy with fish batter and waving flags, and music followed
the whims of the breeze back and forth across the channel.
The foul smells of the waterfront were gone for me now, and
it seemed the creek was in the midst of a magnificent carnival.

Over at Tony Red's, a pair of Bermuda shorts and his be-
jeweled wife were descending the front steps, their faces grim
with concentration after a decadent brunch. The restaurant
facade was a collection of boulders, awnings and palm trees
that quivered in the heat like an art deco mirage.

With the notable exceptions of the bridge and Tony Red's,
nothing on the creek had the look of permanence. Both shores
had been battered by countless storms, and the daily aggressions of wind and salt made young buildings old in a hurry. I
thought perhaps it was that, the reality of accelerated aging,
that made everything on the waterfront seem so acutely alive.

But of course it was also Donna. I had been on the docks a
week, only a week, yet life was so full during those days that
it seemed an entire season. There was no word yet of a boat,
but any impatience I'd had was melting away. It would come
when it would come, and in the meantime I would savor the
wait. Eventually I would learn that waterfront friendships
can burn as brightly and briefly as flashbulbs. But on those
first lovely mornings I was still swaddled in the illusion that
good things, when they are simple, can last.

What Donna and I had doesn't seem simple now. But after
months of slow despair, happiness of any kind had the aura
of impeccable good sense. We knew from the outset that Leo
would still make his visits. There was no indication of when,
or even if, Donna would bless me with her beauty again. We
had enjoyed our lovemaking like the healthy pagans we
were. And when we finished, Donna shimmied playfully like

a stripper before she dressed and skipped down the stairs.
That was—and has remained ever since—the happiest
single moment of my life. It would soon be followed by one of
the worst.

*   *   *

The next morning Donna was running an errand to
Bunny's office when a familiar figure appeared at the door.
His bearing was different, but his face was just as round and
red as I remembered. He walked purposefully to the bar.

"Vun beers, please."

He held up a folded dollar bill like a detective badge. That
summer a dollar was enough for two beers, but I took it he
was asking for one.

"Yes, sir. What kind you need?"

"Please forgive," he said, bowing from the waist.
"Budveizuh, of course."

He measured each step to the patio and adjusted his chair
there with a butler's care. Then he sat at attention, reached
into his shirt, and withdrew the stethoscope.

Yes, it was my old acquaintance from the parking lot, the
man who'd somersaulted onto the oyster shells.

Donna came back, and I motioned to the window. He had
pressed the stethoscope to his chest and was monitoring a se-
ries of deep breaths.

"That guy out there," I said. "Last week I watched him do
an Olga Korbut off the front steps. Who is he?"

"Depends on what day it is. Did he say anything?"

"Vun beers. Budveizuh."

"Oh, that means he's Dr.—what's-his-name—Eric Von
Something. Von Fistfurt, I think. A retired surgeon from some
big shot clinic in Germany."

"Who is he on a bad day?"

"You name it. Sometimes he's Miles Burgess, this million-
aire guy who made his fortune exporting cotton."

That wasn't all. The man with the stethoscope was an astonishing chameleon whose identity changed with every sunrise. For any given appearance he might be LaRue Piedmont, the biplane stunt pilot. Or Melvin Duplantis, the philosophy professor. Or an oil wildcatter named Oran Bowman.

"You've probably guessed," Donna said. "He's only playing with about forty-seven cards."

Out on the patio, though, he exuded the serenity of a Nobel laureate. I had seen a different incarnation in the parking lot—judging by his verbosity then, it must have been the philosopher—yet he was still wearing the stethoscope. I asked Donna if he always carried it.

"Better believe it. That's his pride and joy. He's always doing research, whether he's the doctor or one of the other fellas. The doctor's sort of his main guy, and all the other ones look up to him and help him out.

"I never asked him, but I think he buys a beer for every one of the guys. Keep an eye on him. He's not going to leave until he drinks eight cold ones, one right after the other."

Before long the doctor returned with an empty can in one hand and the two quarters I'd given him in the other. Again he ordered vun beers and walked back to the patio with the precision of an altar boy. I asked Donna who he really was.

"Teddy something. Don't know his last name, but he's harmless enough. Opens oysters for Stimson's, and has as long as I've been here. All I know about him is, well, it's something you won't like."

"Try me."

"Well, he's college, Sam. Till you got here, he was the only one on the docks."

I laughed, but soon felt the wind rush out of me. Would that be me in thirty years, an oyster shucker spooked to madness? I looked out to the creek, where a shrimp boat was chugging by with a modified crab trap on the stern and a nervous, tail-flicking cat inside. My mind whirred like a slide projector—Knuckles' snake, leathery hands, rotting fish, the smoke-stiffened sadness in Tina's curtains. It hit me like ice: I had been kidding myself all along. This place was going to swallow me.

"What's the matter?" Donna said. "Looks like you lost your best friend."

There...there it was, a faint glimmer. At least there was Donna.

"Want me to get you something? You don't look so good, Sam."

I took a deep breath. "It's...nothing—just felt a little weird for a minute."

The front door swung open and a stooped figure limped through. He was a tall man, powerful once but knobbed and stringy now. Had I known at that rickety moment in my life what havoc this man would bring to it, I might have bought a stethoscope and retired immediately to the patio.

But all I saw then was a harmless old porter without the spunk to look anyone in the eye. There were dozens of them on the waterfront, men cowed by the booze and the boss and the pitiless work. He was bent at the shoulder and the waist as though he was uncomfortable with his height, and his pants were cinched with a belt so long that its tongue drooped over his fly.

Donna turned and saw him—and visibly flinched.

"Might as well tell you now," she whispered. "That there's my old man."

I looked back and forth between them like a tennis umpire. Donna had told me her father was dead.

She carried a Lone Star to his table and squatted down beside him. He shrugged a few times as she talked but never took his eyes off his can. She came back to the bar shaking her head.

"Go ahead," she muttered. "Don't bust a gut holding it in."

"What do you mean, your old man?"

"We've been together more than two years."

Together. Two years. Leo. Me.

"Oh," I said.

His attention never drifted from his beer, which he sucked with a toothless baby's devotion. Well, at least he and Donna had one thing in common.

"That there," Donna said, "that's the late, great Fletcher Quinn."

He had the sad, wrinkled eyes of the Irish and the cigar-like texture of a man who had spent his life in the sun. His shoulders were broad but hollow, and his thick fingers were indecisive on the can. But I had to marvel at his hair—a full gray pompadour, dry and brittle now, but trained like a movie star's. I watched his cheeks cave in as he drank, and I blurted out a thought.

"This guy, he's not the one who shoots dentures, is he?"

Donna smiled weakly.

"No, that boy's long gone."

"Does this guy know about that guy?"

"Nope. And he don't know about you. And he don't know about Leo, neither."

I looked at the clock and went cold.

"Oh yeah. The guy who's due here any minute."

"You got it," Donna said. "Wonder if you could find something to do out in the parking lot so you can tell him who's here."

Leo's pickup rolled in just as I was closing the door.

"Got a message," I said numbly. "There's somebody named Fletcher Quinn inside."

"Holy shit." Leo glanced at the door in terror as he shifted to reverse. "Okay, okay. I'm gone. Tell her same time, same—"

He was out of the parking lot before he could finish. The slumped old fellow in the bar was having quite an effect on Tina's lovebirds. All three of them.

Back inside Donna and I exchanged blank expressions while Fletcher studied his beer can. I tried to fathom whether I felt jealous and—even more puzzling—which man it made sense to be jealous of. Finally, in a kind of perverse desperation, I asked Donna if she was going to introduce us.

"Now's as good a time as any," she sighed. "But don't get your hopes up. Fletch ain't exactly Mr. Personality these days."

Donna shuffled ahead and whispered something to him, and I wondered what kinds of intimacies really passed between these two. Fletcher stood unsteadily and glanced at me for a pained second. His handshake was crusty and loose. We sat, and Donna took the chair between us.

"Sam here's a college man," she said. "He's gonna work the dock until we can find him a boat for the summer."

He seemed relieved to hear it.

"Fletcher's got him a boat, Sam, but he's worked by himself ever since I quit him." His pale blue eyes seemed to glaze at that. "He's figured out you don't always have to work if nobody else shows up at the dock every morning."

Donna had mentioned a crewing stint in her past, but never anything about a Fletcher Quinn.

"See, Sam, what happened was, Fletcher decided he didn't want to go out today. He's been out every day for more than a week, and for him that's kind of a record."

She turned toward him.

"So, let me guess, was it the fuel line today, Fletch?"

He shook his head.

"The water pump?"

No.

Donna patted his hand. "Come on, big fella. The suspense is killing us."

"Alternator belt," he said hoarsely. He smiled and blew air through his nose.

"Shoulda known," Donna said. "What it is, Sam, is Fletcher gets lazy sometimes. But he's got a conscience. He don't want to just take the day off and beat the owner out of all that money.

"So he tears up the boat. Just a little bit, mind you, on account of his conscience. Just enough so it's not worth going out that day. Ain't that how it works, Fletch?"

He grinned sheepishly and reached for his beer. The truth was out, and now he could relax. Fletcher pushed back from the table and crossed his legs grandly, as if he were being roasted at a testimonial dinner. But when Donna left to wait on another table, Fletcher and I were left with an awkward silence.

"Tell me," I finally said. "How did you and Donna come to know one another?"

He seemed confused. Donna answered on her way back from the bar.

"When I had my place, Fletch used to be a regular. He was just in from Biloxi then, and he had his own boat."

Fletcher relaxed again and took a long drink. At that moment Donna must have seen him precisely as I did.

"He was a looker in them days, Sam. Used to wear this snappy black commodore's hat. His hair wasn't so gray then, and he wouldn't be caught dead without his teeth."

Fletcher nodded shyly.

"Some people used to say he favored Gregory Peck."

The front door opened again to reveal Jaquita, Sharlene's babysitter, who paused to lean against it in obvious pain. The giant round gauze on her toe was battered and soaked red with blood.

"You gonna have to take the baby," she said in a quivering voice. "One of my boys stepped on my foot, and it's about to drive me blind."

Sharlene skipped through door and, upon seeing Fletcher, erupted in the most delirious "Two!" that her little lungs could manage. She all but flew to our table and into Fletcher's arms.

"Whenever he's around," Donna said matter-of-factly, "she don't know there's anybody else in the room."

Donna rose to help Jaquita down the stairs. Sharlene reached up to rub the stubble on Fletcher's face, and he responded with a wide, pink smile. "She don't like me to shave," he said meekly. Sharlene rounded into a cherubic little ball against his chest. "So, mostly I don't."

We talked between chores—Donna and I, while Fletcher listened—until Sharlene began to breathe slowly in his arms. He seemed to be of two minds when Donna moved the baby to the wicker loveseat by the patio. He clearly loved having her with him, but she was cutting into his drinking motion.

Fletcher eventually rounded off a six-pack without a hint of drunkenness, until Donna casually asked when he planned to fix his boat. Suddenly he slammed his beer down, and a white stream of Lone Star shot three feet into the air and landed in his lap.

"Just asking," Donna said, daubing at his pants with her bar rag. Fletcher sat passively with his arms dangling—and almost immediately fell asleep.

"Let's be out of his way when he comes to," Donna whispered. "He's more likely to go fix the boat if he wakes up alone."

I followed Donna behind the bar. In a few minutes Fletcher's head bobbed and snapped up straight. He rubbed his face, poked at the dampness in his lap, and then limped out the door without looking at anyone.

"Got him all figured out," Donna said happily. She reached for her purse and rang up his tab.

*   *   *

"Poor old Sam. How about we split a sandwich?"

Donna pulled a rubbery hamburger from the microwave and began cutting her half into small chunks. Fletcher had been gone an hour, Dr. Von Fistfurt had stumbled out after his eighth "beers," and Jaquita had returned from the clinic with a fresh golf ball on her toe. I was on a barstool, trying to digest the day's events.

"You look about half addled, Sam." Donna shuffled around the bar and took the stool beside mine. "Ain't no sadder sight than a college man halfway addled."

I wanted to know why Donna had Leo if there was Fletcher, or why Fletcher if there was Leo—or why me if there was either one. But I had too little courage to ask, and certainly no standing to be jealous. I was merely the latest in a long line of fortunates.

And it wasn't as if I hadn't been warned. Bunny told me to

watch out for that Donna—and Donna herself had said as much before she led me upstairs.

No, if anyone had the right to ask, it was Fletcher. He was the one who had committed two years to Donna and helped her raise Sharlene. But Donna apparently had seen to it that he was the only one of her lovers who didn't know there was someone else—unless, of course, there were others out there who were also being fooled.

"Go ahead, Sam. What's on your mind?" Donna now seemed amused, almost eager for me to poke into the wasp nest of her life.

"I guess you were right," I said. "People like me don't know about people like you."

She gave my neck a playful squeeze. "The minute you start understanding—look out. That's when you'll be as crazy as I am."

It was plain that I was light years away from being Donna's significant other. For some reason, that prize had fallen to a gaunt old geezer named Fletcher. He was a curious figure in his own right, but by attracting Donna he became for me an object of fascination. I wanted to know more about him, even if only to reach a deeper understanding of her. So I took a bite of tasteless food and asked Donna to tell me who he was.

"Ah, the incredible Fletcher Quinn," she said. "He's really something, that one. Wouldn't know it to look at him now, but he used to be one of the smoothest guys around here."

"Funny you never mentioned him."

She shrugged matter-of-factly. "Never came up, until now."

True enough—it hadn't. But I thought of Bunny yet again and wondered what other surprises, or hidden dangers, were in store.

"I was running my own bar when I met him. He left Biloxi on account of wife trouble, or so he told me, and I got no reason to doubt it. He says he's got two old wives and two kids back in Mississippi. I don't imagine they know whether he's alive or dead."

Two kids. Fletcher looked too old to be leaving children at home. But I was no judge—I'd only missed Donna's age by two decades.

"Kids?" I said. "How old is he?"

Donna gummed a piece of sandwich and said forty-six. I nodded as though that was my guess.

"I figure he had a middle-aged crazy fit or something. Said he came home one night after he'd spent fourteen hours catching thirty-two pounds of shrimp. His wife got on his butt about how they never had a Christian home for their kids, what with him on the water all the time. So he got right back on his boat and drove it until he couldn't hear her no more. He wound up in Galveston for a while, and then he came in here."

Donna sighed like a teeny-bopper with a crush.

"I gotta tell you, Sam. That man really made a splash when he first came into town. Everybody stopped what they were doing just to have a look at this tall, dark stranger with the black hat. He had this way about him, I don't know, kinda like he was from the movies instead of real life. I still get goose bumps thinking about it.

"I'll never forget this one night. Two drunks were making a ruckus in the bar about who could hold his breath the longest. They had a couple of contests, but one of them kept accusing the other one of sneaking some air. The only way to settle it, they figured, was to do it under water.

"This'll show you how drunk they were—they wound up jumping in the creek with all their clothes on. Now understand, nobody but nobody goes in that creek out there. It's full of diesel and garbage and who knows what all—and it's got currents you wouldn't believe. There's been more than one drunk killed trying to swim across it on a dare. But these boys wouldn't hear it. They were going in, and that was that.

"Before long the contest got to be a big operation, with side bets and bellyaching and all, just like a chicken fight. Everybody piled out the back door to see who was gonna beat who. When everybody got outside, Fletcher had just pulled up and was tying off. And then these fools jumped in the water right behind his boat.

"Pretty soon one of 'em ran out of air and came up, but the other guy just kept stayin' under and stayin' under. It was dark, but I had a light out there and you could see him under the water—his arms were kind of flailin' out to the sides. Finally the other guy went under to pull him up. But he came back up saying, `He's stuck knee-deep in the mud! He's gonna drown if he ain't already!'

"Well, everybody froze in their shoes and stared. Nobody thought to jump in or even say anything. But before you know it, Fletcher just leaned over the back of his boat and, in one motion, reached in and pulled the guy on deck. The fool had to weigh at least two hundred pounds, but Fletcher jerked him out by his collar just as easy as nothing.

"It all happened so fast that nobody knew what to say. Fletcher had only been in town a couple of days, and it was like some hero had ridden in on a horse. Nobody hardly talked about it the rest of the night, but you could tell what everybody was thinking."

Donna smiled sadly.

"Fletcher was bigger than life, Sam. You ain't never seen nothing like it. Soon as those two fools were back onshore and everybody was just staring at him, he flipped in his lines and headed up the creek. Left without saying a word. How could I keep from falling for a man like that?"

I looked at my sandwich, took a deep breath, and wondered if I would ever see Donna throw her jeans on the floor again.

* * *

Late that night I was roused from a lewd dream by the very woman featured in it. Donna was crouched above me in the dark, agitated and breathless, hushing me before I could think clearly enough to speak.

"Be quiet," she whispered. "There's still some people

drinking on the patio. I don't want nobody to know I'm up here."

My eyes came into focus and I saw Sharlene, groggily sucking her thumb at Donna's side.

"He got all drunked up," Donna said, checking the window. "Hell, he's been drinking since seven this morning. And then he got into some whiskey. He never could handle whiskey, Sam, not after he's been drinking all day."

"What happened?"

"Oh, never mind that. But you've got to help me, okay?"

"Sure—of course. Are you alright?"

"I'm fine. But I had to get me and the little rascal out of there. We tried sleeping in the car, but it's so damn hot. And little queenie here, she can't sleep without she's got a fan on her.

"I didn't have the nerve to wake up Jaquita again, especially with her bad toe and all. So I was wondering, Sam, would you mind it if she stayed with you tonight?"

"Don't be ridiculous. Of course it's alright."

"If it comes up, I'll tell him I left her at Jaquita's. He won't bother her, on account of he knows how hard it is to get a good babysitter." She crouched down and whispered to the girl. "Go ahead, pistol, crawl up into bed with Sam."

Sharlene was snuggled against me in seconds. Donna leaned over to kiss each of us on the cheek, then turned for the door.

"Wait a minute," I said. "Where are you going?"

"Oh, I don't know. Somewhere, anywhere he can't find me until he's got his head screwed on straight."

"Uh-uh. You're staying here."

She shook her head firmly. "No, I wouldn't do that to you, Sam. You have no idea…"

"But Donna—"

"Hush now, I've got to go. I don't want him driving by and seeing my car here. See you in the morning."

Before I could speak again, Donna blew me a hurried kiss and vanished dówn the stairs.

Seven

Sharlene soon fell into the deep slumber of the innocent, but I spent the night staring at the ceiling. My mind raced from one ugly scenario to another until finally, Donna returned to open the bar—and confirmed one of my worst fears.

She avoided me at first, but as the sun rose there was no hiding the damage done to her left eye. It was swollen and watery, with the first hints of purple already rising from the cheekbone. Eventually she acknowledged the obvious and tried to force a laugh.

"Come on, Sam, it's just a shiner. Ain't you never seen a shiner before?"

"Never on you," I said. "That son of a bitch..."

"Now, don't make a big deal about it. I got an idea he's gonna have a nice one, too."

"Jeez, Donna."

"He was drunk and feeling sorry for himself. I shoulda let him alone. Hell, it's my fault as much as his."

"Don't say that. I don't care if—"

"Look, Sam. Deep down he's a good man, a real good one. Sometimes he lashes out at his bad luck, that's all. And sometimes I don't have sense enough to get out of the way."

"There's no excuse for this, Donna."

She shook her head dismissively, and my anger began to rise. "Look, it's not just you. What about Sharlene?"

"He didn't touch her, Sam."

"Maybe not this time. And besides, she shouldn't be seeing things like that."

"Oh, hell. She don't even know what's going on half the time."

"That leaves the other half."

Donna was losing patience with this, but I pressed ahead anyway. "Kids pick up more than you realize. The idea that he would hit you—and that she could see that—well, it just makes me sick."

"It's not like it happens every day."

"Doesn't matter. Once is too often, Donna."

She turned to walk away, then stopped herself. "You don't know!" she shouted, giving in suddenly to tears. "That man...he's just...you didn't know him before, Sam. He's lost so much...and he's got nothing left but me and her. He's a good man, deep down. He really is. And I feel so goddamn sorry..."

I tried to embrace her, but she pulled away. "I owe him, Sam. I owe him so much. And Sharlene, she worships the ground he walks on. Things aren't...it's not as simple as you think it is."

Sharlene emerged from under the pool table and stared wide-eyed at Donna.

"Now, look what we've done." Donna managed a pained laugh. "Poor thing. You don't want to see me cry, do you? Come on over here, baby, and give me some lovin'."

Sharlene moved tentatively forward, then wrapped herself around Donna's leg.

"Attagirl," Donna said, smoothing the hair on Sharlene's forehead. "Everthing's gonna be fine, just fine. Sam don't know it yet, but everything's gonna be fine..."

*   *   *

The black eye seemed to have a liberating effect on Donna, who began to talk more freely about herself than ever before.

For dark reasons that would soon become all too clear, she was eager—almost desperate—to convince me of Fletcher's good will.

During our idle hours together she disclosed thoughts that a shrimper never would have—and in ways she never would have with a shrimper. The stories came slowly and haltingly at first, with every disclosure measured against its risks. But within days she was relating the most personal details of her past, even reenacting bedroom conversations with her lover.

At times I felt the melancholy of a court eunuch in whom the queen confides the intimacies of the throne. I never lost interest. Donna and Fletcher's history was compelling, and it bore directly on my standing with her. But I didn't like what my access to these secrets said about me.

*   *   *

For Fletcher Quinn—and so, for Donna—life after his grand entrance on the creek had been a long and harrowing fall. The man who once captained his own boat was reduced to sabotaging someone else's for a day off. Fletcher had swept Donna off her feet only two years before, and now she was struggling to keep him on his.

Donna and Fletcher became an official item within days of his heroics at the dock. And by the cool social measurements of the waterfront, they were a glamorous item at that. He was the inscrutable new paladin, she the beloved owner of the bar most favored by the lords of the bay. Fletcher and Donna were drawn to one another naturally, with few words, during what they both regarded as the prime of their lives.

Donna showed me a photograph, scavenged from the Falcon's glove compartment, of the two of them holding court in her waterfront beer joint. Fletcher's black hat was there, propped carelessly on the side of his head, and he smiled at the camera with a bemused tolerance. He had a shiny set of teeth in those days. Donna said she never saw him without his dentures until he lost so much weight they didn't fit anymore. But that would come later. In the height of his glory Fletcher was a strapping, squinty-eyed marvel with a boat of his own and the lady of his choice tucked under his arm.

The Polaroid was not so kind to Donna. She, too, had a white smile then, but somehow the act of smiling made her eyes look sad. The teased bubble from her driver's license was there, too, and her arms were fleshier than they were when I met her.

The biggest surprise was Donna's posture. She hunched under Fletcher with her hands between her knees, seemingly cowed by her man. Yet this was the same woman whose fierce eyes had startled me when we met. And this was Fletcher, the man who could now fall asleep with beer in his lap.

Donna's bar had been even more a shrimper's hangout than Tina's Marina, where the patio view attracted some drinkers with no connection to the creek. But Donna's Place—naming it had been easy—was tucked among the fish houses on the docks beneath the bridge. It was a neighborhood bar where everyone knew everyone. Dogs slept under tables, and kids played outside among the stilts.

Fletcher lived on his boat, and Donna kept a room behind the bar. Their romance blossomed in her room after hours, and it was only a matter of days before they chafed at containing their ardor until closing time. Then one evening, while she and Fletch were floating in midnight's afterglow, Donna offered a solution.

"Been thinking," she whispered. "We're always saying how hard it is to wait till closing time to be alone."

Fletcher nodded at the ceiling.

"Well, Suzanne can run the place awhile when I'm gone. Then you and me can sneak off to your boat."

He sat up in the darkness and looked out to the dock. Donna couldn't see the boat from where she lay, but she pictured it...freshly painted white, with wavy light glinting on the hull. She reached for Fletcher's back, and it felt tight as a cat's. She knew immediately what was wrong.

"Sorry, Fletch. Bad idea."

Donna shrank farther under the sheet and faced the first disappointment about her new lover. Fletcher was one of the fervent captains, an obsessive shrimper whose attachment to his boat bordered on the sexual. It was everything...the place where he defined himself, expressed his worth, found sanctuary from the mundane hordes on shore. Some shrimpers could dock their boats and forget about them until morning, but men like Fletcher were tied umbilically to theirs.

"Don't get me wrong," he finally said. "It ain't nothing personal. But there's never been a woman on my boat. Not either one of my wives, not nobody. It...it just wouldn't be right."

Fletcher, to his credit, had the presence to see his disease—and the kindness to make it up to Donna. He came to the bar every night, after showering in a fish house, and stayed with his lady until the back room was theirs again. Some nights they left Donna's Place to go dancing. Sometimes they hopped other bars along the creek. They had late suppers at a cafe in San Leon and occasionally on the seawall in Galveston.

But always, no matter the day or the week, they were barred from Donna's room until midnight. As weeks turned into months, the arrangement became more and more a burden.

Then one afternoon Fletcher announced he had bought a repossessed trailer home, putting up his boat in lieu of a down payment. Life was cozy for months. He was within walking distance of his boat, she just a short hop from her bar. The money flowed, good times rolled, and it seemed the magic would never end.

Until the storm came. It was a gale, with only half the punch of a hurricane. But it was angry enough to separate Donna's Place from most of its pilings. She had leased the building from a retired accountant who decided he was weary of repairs. In a matter of hours, Donna became a merchant without a shop.

Fletcher stayed ashore the next morning to help Donna

gather the few fixtures worth saving. He was lifting the cash register when the floor gave way. He fell eight feet to the oyster shell outside and was trapped under a beam for more than an hour. When the fire department finally pulled him free, his hip was crushed and six inches of his right thighbone were sticking through his pants. From that moment, nothing in either of their lives would be the same.

*   *   *

Weeks passed before Donna could drive him home from the hospital. Fletcher's cast forced him to lie across the back seat like a man in an iron lung. She made a few cheerful attempts at conversation. He looked at the upholstery. Then he carried a six-pack from the refrigerator to the bedroom and started drinking before he hit the mattress. Donna waited a few hours before she tried again.

When she tiptoed in that night, the bedroom had the sweet, sticky aroma that her bar took on when someone spilled beer. Fletcher was asleep under the cans with his mouth open, and Donna winced at what she saw. In their time together she had never been permitted to view him without his teeth. Now she was suddenly in the presence of an old man with soft, pink little gums. The hollows in his cheeks made his nose grow, and his skin sagged like candle wax.

Fletcher stirred, and Donna's expression made him remember his mouth. She found an excuse to turn away while he fumbled for his dentures.

"How you doin, Fletch? I guess the pain pills and the beer helped you sleep."

He took a slow breath. Even with his teeth in, the lines on his face were deeper than Donna remembered. Everything—his skin, his eyes, his hair—was blanched a shade lighter.

"Anything I can get you?"

He breathed again.

"Hey, now. It's me here."

Fletcher's face turned slowly away, and Donna knew she was losing control of her life.

"Tell me if I'm wrong," she whispered. "You're worried, I know. You're wondering how you're gonna work the boat this way."

Donna took his hand and was startled by the timorous squeeze he gave her.

"Fletch. You know it's gonna be all right. You'll just be in the cast awhile, and then you'll be back to normal."

"Months," he croaked. "I ain't gonna be worth a damn for months."

"Months, then. It ain't the end of the world."

"What are we gonna do? I got doctor bills out my ass. Your bar's gone, and there's a pile of debts on it. We've never had no savings, you know that. We're gonna lose the trailer, if we don't starve first."

"Wait a minute, Fletch. There's a lot of things you're forgetting here. I can get a job—there's always somebody that can use a barmaid. And you, you can hire someone to run your boat until you're stronger."

Fletcher groaned and closed his eyes.

"Just great," he said. "My woman hustlin' tips to support me while I sit on my ass and let somebody tear my boat to shit. Ain't nobody worth his piss gonna take a boat for just a few weeks."

"But Fletch—"

"Nobody runs my boat but me! You got that?"

It was the last flicker of heat Donna would feel in her man for months. Fletcher wasn't educated, but he knew precisely what he was. Strength was all that mattered in his world—who had it and who didn't, who squandered it and who used it well. Fletcher's extraordinary power had let him stand astride the waterfront while everyone else flailed and bickered at his feet.

But it was all slipping away. Weeks of drinking beer on his back softened Fletcher's chest and shoulders. The cast took away his strut, and the pain pills clouded his brain. Everything chipped away at his ability to command, until he had fallen so far he couldn't even remember how it felt to be at the summit.

Donna's gay months with Fletcher did nothing to prepare her for his decline, and the speed of it numbed her. But she cared for him, brought his Lone Star, helped him to the toilet. More and more decisions fell to her. As the money pressures mounted, his interest in them waned. Finally, something had to give. The bank was making moves to take the trailer.

Donna watched Fletcher snore one afternoon—he was leaving his dentures out more often now—and tried to decide on a path. If she signed on as a barmaid it would surely grease Fletcher's skids, and the same was true of hiring a skipper for his boat. But it was clear Fletcher couldn't run the boat alone, and no reliable deck hand would take a job under him now. She looked at his pink gums and his sinking chest and found herself shaking him awake.

"Listen, damn you, here's how it's going to be. We're gonna run your boat together. You're well enough to steer it now, and I'm strong enough to crew it. You just tell me what needs doing, and it'll get done."

Donna remembered the tightness in his back the night she'd suggested they slip onto the boat together. But now she was saying it again, and she was going to keep on saying it until it did some good.

"We're not going to quit, you understand? There's gonna be a woman on your boat whether you like it or not, and by God, she's gonna help you run it."

She held her breath and waited. Fletcher stared blankly at the ceiling and licked his gums.

"Well, Fletch, what's it gonna be? You gonna go along with this peaceful, or do I got to beat it out of you?"

He closed his eyes and started to form a word. Donna leaned closer and heard him whisper, "Whatever." And then he was asleep.

Eight

To this day I am convinced there was no better place for my post-graduate study than Tina's Marina. And of course those quiet afternoons with Donna were a sweet and soothing balm. But as my first week on the waterfront stretched into two and then three, I began to grow restive with the daily routines on shore. Donna always assured me that something would come up soon, but every shrimp boat that passed was a reminder that I had stopped short of my goal.

One afternoon a bull-necked little shrimper named Billy Taylor burst into the marina. He headed straight for the men's room and thunked down the toilet seat before the door could close behind him. I looked at Donna expecting a wisecrack, but she seemed to be in agony.

"Hey, Sam," she said suddenly. "Is the cooler stocked? Daisy's gonna be coming on pretty soon."

I was puzzled, because we'd just done that an hour before.

"You must have been sleepwalking," I said. "There's hardly room for another can."

"How about the bathrooms? Did we get those yet?"

No, we hadn't. I headed for the supply closet and stepped aside for Billy, still zipping his pants. Donna handed him a can and glanced at me before she busied herself with the bar rag.

"Hey," he finally growled. "Ain't you gonna ast me how come I'm home so early?"

Donna looked nervous. She was trying to ignore him.

"Sam," she said, "could you go ask Bunny for some quarters? She'll be gone when Daisy needs 'em."

I picked up the water bucket slowly. Something was very wrong.

"I'll tell ya how come I'm early. It's that damned deckhand you sent me."

I felt the weight of the bucket in my forearm, my shoulder, my neck. The sounds of the bar grew tinny.

"Sumbitch got seasick. Puked all over the goddamn boat— and I mean all over it. Half the time he couldn't even make it to the side."

"Billy, that's—"

"I'm talkin' puke on the deck, puke on the winch, puke on the baskets, puke everywhere. He even put it all over my bunk when he tried to lay down. My boat stinks like Skid Goddamn Row."

Donna started folding her bar rag. There was nothing she could do now.

"Had to do all the damn cullin' myself, and I was washing more vomit through the scuppers than I was fish. Finally had to come back before the fool died on me."

Donna wouldn't look up. Billy grinned at me for a reaction.

"So..." I said.

Donna looked at me and tried to shake her head without letting Billy see.

"Tell me," I said. "Does that mean you need a deckhand?"

"Naw, not yet. Poor bastard says he usually takes some kind of seasick medicine. Only he forgot it on account of it being his first day and all."

I was beginning to taste something bitter.

"Gonna give him another chance, I guess. Wouldn't do it, but Donna told me he's a good boy."

I stared down at the bucket and just couldn't feature myself scrubbing these toilets anymore. I dropped it in a loud splash and turned for the dock.

"Sam!" Donna shouted. "I need to talk to you."

I slammed the door without looking back and wished only that I'd stayed long enough to spit in her lying face.

* * *

When I closed the door on Donna all I knew was that I had to keep moving. Sitting in my room would have been the same as asking her to come up and explain everything away. No, I'd heard enough lies for one summer. Before my eyes could react to Maxwell's glare I was across the street in the Texas Paradise, a plywood beer joint painted pink and frog-skin green. I resolved to do what any decent idiot would in my situation—drink to the point of paralysis.

I took the table nearest the window and glared at Tina the Mermaid, who was still smiling radiantly. She didn't give a damn about me or my troubles. And neither, it was clear, did Donna.

"What's it gonna be, Hoss?" The barmaid squinted at me. "Hey, ain't you the dock hand over at Rodney Gene's?"

I didn't know anymore, but I wasn't up to discussing it.

"Bring me a Schlitz."

"How come you're drinking beer over here in the middle of the afternoon?"

Before I realized it, I'd shot her a look that made her retreat to the bar. But six ounces into my first can I was beginning to calm down. The Paradise was a sedative on stilts, a warm place with big shutters thrown open to the sun. Behind me, three old men and a boy were playing dominoes in the shade between two windows. Now and then I heard the crack of pool balls in the back room.

Why had I trusted her? The very morning I met Donna, she broke into my room. Then in the long afternoons when I thought we were scraping the crust from our hearts, she gave me a life story that omitted the man she'd been living with for two years. All of that about her parents, her teeth, her beer joint. It was no more believable now than if I'd heard it from

Dr. Von Fistfurt.

She was using me. Having a dimwit to run the bar meant she and Leo could have their lunchtime workouts upstairs. Finding me a boat would destroy that little arrangement. Donna and I hadn't gone to my room together since our first encounter, but I'd foolishly blamed that on shortages of time and opportunity. Now it was clear she was stringing me along for as long as I stayed stupid.

One beer quickly begat another, and my head began to spin in the heat. Over and over came the invasive thought that *Donna didn't care.* The notion had never occurred to me before, but there I was, damaged past the point of screaming because *Donna didn't care.* Until Billy Taylor showed up, there was always the possibility, the buried fantasy, that Donna might one day see me as central to her life. And then it came to me: It wasn't the lies that mattered, not the games, not even losing the boat. What hurt most was the stark fact that Donna meant more to me than I did to her.

Outside, Daisy drove into the parking lot and struggled out of her battered Pontiac. I wondered what she would hear when she asked Donna where I was. A sudden illness, maybe, or an errand that couldn't wait. Then again, Donna and Daisy were close enough that they might laugh that the little twerp had finally caught on.

The door closed behind Daisy, and Bunny's ride pulled up, two hours ahead of schedule. The big man in the black pickup was crushing beer cans again. Bunny forced her wobbly ankles across the shell and then looked back toward Tina as the truck rolled away. No slippery greeting for the big man this time. Maybe she was thinking of the young dock hand inside.

The barmaid brought a fresh beer and tried again. "So, how you liking it over at the marina?" Her small mouth made her look angry.

"Not much," I groused. "What I really want is a job on a boat."

She flipped a black thumbnail in Tina's direction.

"I guess you know that's where all the men go to get one."

"So I hear."

"Donna knows about all the captains they is on the bay. She's the one who can help you."

I took a long draught of Schlitz to close the conversation. Donna would be leaving soon, and I didn't want any distractions. Eventually she opened the door and saw my car in the parking lot, then knocked on my apartment door a couple of times. She opened her purse for the key, then thought better of it.

She came back to the parking lot, taut with worry. I knew much about Leo that she didn't want Bunny—or Fletcher—to hear. She glanced at the Paradise and her eyes seemed briefly to meet mine, but she couldn't see beyond the shiny screen between us. Eventually she threw her purse into her Falcon and drove away. It was good knowing she felt a measure of agony, too.

Out on the creek, in the gap between the marina and Tony Red's, a shrimper was coming in. The deck hand was on the foredeck, savoring a cigarette. He had the seat I wanted, but now my hopes of working on the water were smoldering. The shrimpers were unapproachable, and my only link to them was gone.

Already I was twenty-one years old. At my age, Melville was hunting whales, outrunning cannibals. And I didn't have what it took to make day trips on a shrimp boat.

When the Schlitz and the visions of Typee finally became too much, I slipped outside for some air. Corbin's Bar & Grill was within stumbling distance, and it offered the solace of coffee and french fries. I made my way inland, distracted for a few more precious seconds from the matter of what I would do with my life.

* * *

Corbin's was a diner with an adjacent beer joint, but its red-brick facade gave it the look of a sewage lift station. In the cafe, two men were drinking coffee at the counter, trying to ignore the music blaring from the juke box next door.

I took a booth and had just scalded my tongue when Bunny burst through the swinging doors from the bar. She saw me, then spun coquettishly into the restroom, her thick forefinger ordering me to wait until she was finished. She didn't take long.

"Hey, Sam!" she shouted. "Got room for some company? You look so sad sitting here all by your lonesome."

I watched her struggle onto the bench across from me. The waitress seemed amused when she dropped off my hamburger basket, but Bunny ordered a beer in a tone that wiped her smile away.

"Tell me, Sam, how you liking things at the marina?"

There was that question again. Had she seen me leave that afternoon? Was I about to be fired?

"Fine," I said.

"That's good. But how come you never come see me? A girl gets lonely, cooped up in that office all day."

My next bite tasted a little better. "Well," I said blandly, "Donna gets out there sometimes…"

"Screw Donna," she snapped. "Screw her and dump her in the trash."

I heard myself laugh out loud. Only a few hours before, that wouldn't have happened.

Bunny licked her lips. "You keep to yourself pretty much, don't you? Nice young fella like you orta circulate more."

The waitress delivered Bunny's Lone Star. I suddenly imagined myself being crushed in one hand.

"Where's that big guy I saw the other day?"

Bunny swallowed hard and suppressed a burp.

"Who's that, honey?"

"You know. The guy in the pickup who treats beer cans like gum wrappers. He wouldn't be next door by any chance?"

"Nope. He's back at the house, working on his truck. I'm all by my little ol' self." She propped her elbow against a bulbous breast and held her beer can aloft.

"C'mon, Sam, talk to me. How you likin' that room? The job suit you? Whatcha think of all the low-lifes on the docks?"

I began to feel a guilty regret over the distance I'd kept between myself and Bunny. For all her faults, she was ultimately a sad creature—and the one person on the docks who seemed genuinely concerned about me and my welfare. In return, I'd treated her as icily as the shrimpers treated me.

"Everything would be fine," I said, "if I could just find a boat."

"Donna ain't got you nothing, that it?"

I took a deep breath, the way skydivers do before they jump.

"Something strange happened today. I found out a guy needed a deck hand, and Donna put him on to somebody else. All along she's been saying I'd get the first chance."

Bunny sniffed and tugged at a bra strap.

"Sounds like something that bitch would pull. Let me tell you about Donna. Don't never turn your back on her, if you get my meaning."

It still made me a little queasy to hear something like that said about Donna. But I didn't argue.

"I wouldn't trust that girl far as I could throw her. She's trouble, Sam, trouble. Just like everything and everybody on those goddamn docks."

I motioned to the waitress. It was time to go back on Schlitz patrol.

"I mean it, Sam. Donna's no better than the rest of 'em. Can I tell you something? I was worried as hell when you turned up and said you wanted on a boat. I imagine you've got this neat picture of what it's gonna be like, the life of the sea and all that shit.

"But you don't know what you're getting into. Just look at those people and think for a minute."

I felt my shoulders sink. They really were a different breed, these men, and there was no way I'd fit in. They seemed to size me up in seconds: skinny arms, smooth face, delicate hands. I wouldn't hire a guy like me to fish the bay. Why should they?

"Tell you what," Bunny said. "If you want to work on the water so bad...do you know the Kingfisher?"

Yes, I did. It was the excursion boat that docked under the bridge. It took kids and their grandmothers out to fish.

"I know the guy that owns it. And the captain, him and his wife are real good friends of mine. He's been telling me how he needs a deck hand bad, now that the tourist season's picking up."

Tourists. I'd heard the snarls in the marina every time the Kingfisher floated by. It was a dude boat, a gaudy pleasure craft that catered to the soft, ignorant hordes from the outside.

"Thanks, Bunny, really. But I didn't come here to bait hooks for the pep squad."

Bunny emptied her can and smacked it on the table.

"You wanna be one of the tough guys, huh? Work for some ignorant captain for half the money you'd make on the Kingfisher?"

I looked up.

"That's right. When school lets out, you're gonna make more on that boat than any damn shrimping deck hand. Only it'll be clean, human work."

I slurred something incoherent. Despair was taking the strength from my voice.

"Tell you what," she said, "Don't decide now. You just sit right there while I go make some phone calls. Soon's I track him down we can go talk it over. No harm in that, is there?"

She blew through the swinging doors to the beer joint before I could form an answer. I looked down at my half-eaten hamburger and pushed it away. Suddenly there was a blur, and I felt two tiny hands over my eyes.

"We finally found you," Donna said. "Somebody wants you to guess who it is."

Sharlene's excited breath stirred my hair, and I pictured her standing in the booth behind me. I was beginning to come to life again.

"Let's see." I was smiling in spite of myself. "Could it be Knuckles?"

Sharlene gurgled happily. Donna told me to guess again.

"Well, it must be Jackie Onassis."

"Two!"

"No, Sam, but you're getting warm."

"Wait a minute. Who else is there?"

"Two! Two!"

"Is it Sharlene?"

She threw her arms around my neck and smothered my head with kisses. I'd made a habit of tagging along with Donna to the babysitter after work. Sharlene and I had become fast friends.

"She missed you at Jaquita's." Donna was still lingering behind me. "I missed you too, Sam."

Sharlene scrambled around to my lap while Donna went to the counter for a beer. I touched one of the girl's lovely ears and asked if she'd had supper yet. Her pearl earrings glinted when she shook her head.

"You like fries?" I held one up, and she opened her mouthlike a hungry chick. "Okay, okay. They're all yours." Sharlene pulled the basket to her and reached in with both hands.

I turned toward Donna and looked over for some kind of message in her eyes. She was cool and awake, not smiling, just waiting at the counter with her arms crossed. She was barefoot now, and she'd let her hair down, straight and shiny around her shoulders. She seemed younger, somehow softer.

Donna took her beer and leveled her eyes at me as she crossed the room. Freed from her sandals, she walked with a muscular certainty, rolling her hips now instead of gripping the floor with her toes.

"Didn't get a chance to say bye," she said wryly. She folded a leg under herself in the booth. "I feel bad about what happened, Sam."

She raised her arms to push her hair back, and I was emboldened to study her T-shirt. Her shoulders and breasts flexed impressively as she moved.

"Well," she said, "ain't you gonna chew my ass?"

That touched off a torrent in me. The plans, the wasted time, the slippery ice of my life...Donna, you magnificent bitch, how could you do this to me?

"God damn you," I snapped. "You knew what I wanted, and you knew I was counting on you."

"Should have let me explain, Sam."

"Don't tell me what I should and shouldn't—you, of all people. You've fed me so much bullshit, it's all I can taste."

Donna watched Sharlene slip her hand into a pool of ketchup. Her eyes were such a clear light gray that the pupils seemed magnified. Indeed, they *were* too large, and I realized she wasn't on her first beer.

"I'll tell you why I done it, Sam. You can believe it or you can forget it. That's up to you."

I waited.

"Billy told me he needed a hand. And yes, I put him onto somebody else. Know why? He's a goddamn thief, that's why. He steals from the owner, steals from the fish house. And you, he woulda stole a guy like you blind. Sam, you deserve better than that asshole."

The story made sense, but I knew Donna wouldn't give me one that didn't. And I realized I was taking shorter breaths.

"So you decided all this for me?"

She nodded unsteadily.

"You were just looking out for old Sam?"

She nodded again.

"And this time I'm supposed to believe it."

She started to nod and stopped herself. Her eyes caught fire.

"Donna, I don't know what to think anymore. I just know I'm tired of being lied to. You want to know what I really think? I think maybe you were just stringing me along so you and Leo could have a house boy."

"You do?"

"Damn straight."

Now I was the liar. I had seen what the accusation did to her, and I knew instantly it couldn't be true. But she had other crimes to pay for.

"Then what am I doing here, Sam?" She looked quickly around the diner. "Why would I come looking for you?"

"House boys must be hard to come by."

Donna laughed bitterly.

"You must not think very much of me, Sam. If I was only worried about myself, I wouldn't have found you another boat."

I felt dizzy. "You what—"

"That's right. Roy Pile fueled up after you left and said he's tired of working by himself, now that it's getting hot. I told him not to hire anybody till I tried to find you."

I couldn't stay in my seat. Sharlene's attention never left her french fries as I slipped her off my lap.

"Where? Where is he? Where do I go?"

Donna pulled a slip of paper from her back pocket.

"He put his address on this."

I crumpled the sheet and squeezed her wrist so hard I must have left fingerprints.

"Is this for real?"

"Real as it gets, sailor. I imagine you ought to hustle over there before he finds somebody else."

My eyes were brimming when I stooped to kiss Donna on the cheek. She looked up suddenly and I felt her soft, wrinkled lips. We both pulled awkwardly away.

"I, I'm sorry, Donna. Sorry for everything."

"Don't worry over it. Just stop dawdlin' with me and go get you a shrimp boat."

Nine

Roy Pile's note, scratched in a shaky and almost indecipherable hand, said he lived south of the Maxwell sewer plant.

For the moment at least, that location wasn't as unfortunate as it seemed. Anyone living south of the waterfront had an easier time in the summer, when the southerly Gulf breeze carried all the stinks toward Adelia. Maxwell was the loser only during the brief northern winds of winter.

I turned at the designated billboard and followed a pair of tire ruts down a lush path. Pile's property wasn't far from the bridge and its traffic, but it was so dense with brush that it seemed plucked from the Kentucky foothills. Trees arched overhead to hide the sky. Back in the shade, an ancient gasoline pump with rounded shoulders stood among the weeds like a mummy. I came to a clearing where a long, green shrimp net drooped from the limbs of a tree. Shielded as it was from the breeze, the place had the hot, damp smell of a compost.

The ruts led eventually to a beige trailer on cinder blocks. At the front door I tried a few times to make my knocks heard over a blaring game show. Then I hopped off the steps to look for another entrance. At that moment Pile appeared, slow and dour, rubbing his stomach though an unbuttoned shirt. He looked down on me like a basset hound reviewing his latest bowel movement.

"Roy Pile?" I said.

He nodded once and leaned on the doorknob.

"I'm Samuel Traynor. Donna told me you're looking for a deck hand."

His eyebrows began to twitch.

"So you're the boy she's so high on," he rumbled. "This gonna be your first time on a boat, I guess."

"Yes, but I spent a lot of time around the water in Fort Worth. I'll work as hard as I can, and I'm sure I'll catch on fast."

His eyebrows kept twitching. Pile was in his sixties, and his face sagged off his jaws. He had a dry, pebbly nose that was swollen by the sun to what must have been twice its original size.

"You're gonna catch on fast."

"Yes, sir."

I started to climb the stairs, until he leaned even more heavily on the door. His soft white belly slumped out farther over his pants.

"Well, I guess I can teach you a few things. Main thing is you gotta show up on time every day. I ain't gonna waste my mornings waiting on no deck hand."

He surveyed my frame with a palpable lack of enthusiasm. "Donna says I can count on you. She right about that?"

"Absolutely."

"All right then, be down to the boat at five-thirty."

The door was closed and locked before I could thank him. Then I realized I didn't know where to go. He answered the door again with the same blank expression.

"Sorry, but I don't know how to find your boat."

"It's the Silver Dollar," he said. "Tied up at Cutter's."

He closed the door on the last syllable, and I let the words tumble around in my head like dice. Then the door reopened suddenly, and his eyebrows were jumping more than ever.

"One thing," he said. "Next time you get yourself a hair-cut, try sitting a little closer to the barber."

The door swung shut again. I ran my hands through my

hair and sucked in the wild smell of success. Every tree, every weed, every blade of grass was waving its congratulations. Life from now on would be a shaded hammock on a lazy afternoon.

* * *

On the way back to the creek, I passed a familiar black pickup outside a beer joint. I realized only then that I had left the diner without seeing Bunny—and without warning Donna she was there. There probably had been an ugly scene, and the blame for it rested solely with me. At the very least, I owed it to Bunny to stop in and apologize—and to tell her I was prepared to vacate my room in the attic.

At the top of the stairs, I took a deep breath. The big boy was sitting next to Bunny with a beer can hidden in his fist. I pictured him lifting me from the floor with that hand and crushing my brain stem with any two fingers on it.

"Bunny," I said meekly. "I hope you'll accept my apology."

"Fuck," she snapped. "Whasha want 'pologize for?" The bagged bottle on the table before her had already taken its toll.

"For this afternoon—"

"Oh yeah, when you ran off and let me show my ass to that fuckin' bish."

"I'm afraid I got so excited about the shrimping job, I forgot you were trying to help. I'm so sorry."

"Thaz okay. Willard here managed to pull the knife out my back."

Her boyfriend looked at me sympathetically.

"I've got no excuse," I said. "It's just that this is a dream come true for me. I couldn't pass it up."

Willard extended a giant arm across the table. "Don't believe we've met," he said in a surprisingly tiny voice. "I'm Willard Dorsey."

He was merciful with my hand.

"So you're gonna work on a shrimp boat, huh? I'm sure

you'll like it."

"Shaddup," Bunny said. "Don't encourage the bashtard."

He looked at me secretly, as if to say, "You understand why I can't help you."

"Bunny, you really have been good to me since I've been here, and I do appreciate it. But please understand this is something I've got to do. I promise I'll be out of the attic in a day or two."

Bunny emptied her glass, then tried in vain to muffle a burp.

"Oh, fuck it," she said. "You can keep the goddamn room, if you pay some rent. Rodney Gene will be thrilled to finally make some money on the place."

I thanked her until she told me to shaddup, and then I started thanking Willard. I ordered a round for the three of us. Bunny sneered at the gesture, but Willard nodded at me when he was sure Bunny couldn't see.

"Since it was my fault, I hope you don't come down too hard on Donna. It wasn't anything against you. She was just doing what I'd asked the first day I got here."

Bunny took a noisy swig from her glass and laughed bitterly.

"Oh yeah...Donna. You thought she was the bish of all bishes this afternoon, didn't ya?"

"That was a misunderstanding."

"I don't get it. Everybody's so goddamn wild about Donna. All I ever hear is Donna this and Donna that. Meet somebody and tell them you work at the marina, and the first thing you hear is, `How's Donna?' All she ever does is flirt with every man she sees. And me, I'm stuck out in that goddamn office all day."

Bunny fumbled for a cigarette, bending it as she brought it to her mouth. "Story of my fucking life," she said, and suddenly her eyes began to redden. "Always in the goddamn background, always shut out of everthing." She lit the cigarette and threw the flaming match to the floor. "I know nobody likes me. It's always been that way. But you'd think I'd fucking get used to it, you know?"

She smudged away a black mascara tear and poured another drink. "Once, just once, I'd like to be the center of something—the star, know what I mean? Sam, you're a college boy. You know what I mean, don't you?"

Willard tried to lighten the mood. "It's not so bad," he said. "I thought you didn't want to go near that marina."

Bunny slapped her glass to the table. "Goddamn right I don't. I know shit about them people that would scorch Sam's eyebrows—stories about Donna, too.

"She's damn lucky she and Rodney Gene are buddies. But she better not fuck up at the marina to where I can prove it, I'll tell you that. I'll fire her ass so fast it'll make her head spin. And she knows it, too."

Bunny burped so loudly that her breasts quivered. I started planning a polite departure.

"You don't believe me, Sam, do you? You just think I'm a crazy old bat."

I shook my head, but with too little conviction. If only I'd been a better actor at that moment, I might have spent a lifetime in blissful ignorance.

"God, Sam, you're so damn blind. But I've got news for you, buddy boy.

"That kid you're so in love with, that Sharlene—that ain't Donna's kid at all. That baby is stolen."

*   *   *

Cutter's Marina was just east of the bridge on the Maxwell side, opposite the Kingfisher. It wasn't much of a place—just a couple of stubbed piers with room for a dozen boats.

The Silver Dollar was a little longer than most bay shrimpers, about forty feet overall. It was well-kept and newly rigged, with a white hull and shiny blue trim. I stood at the beam and watched the moon glisten on a damp strand of chain overhead.

What do you mean, stolen?

That's all I'm saying. I don't want no part of it.
You mean she kidnapped her?
What do you think? You go ask her, if you love her so much.

I followed a stern line from the transom to a piling on the dock beside me. A roach was flitting up the pole to safety, chased from the waterline by a small surge in the tide. The bug stopped, its antennae moving like lightless beacons, and dug in against a puff of wind.

I had to see it from Donna's side. I didn't know the first thing about this place, about her world. She wasn't evil—she was hanging by her fingernails, trying to stay alive until tomorrow. People like me, people on the outside, we couldn't understand...

An outsider would have gone straight to the phone and brought the outside thundering in. But my place in the world had already started to change. And I sat on the dock, alone with the water roach, watching the moon float higher in the sky.

Ten

The sun was still far below the horizon when I returned to the Silver Dollar the next day. I admired the boat's broad shoulders and began tingling with a new awareness. Everything was closer now. There was something reassuring about the weight of my deck boots, the warmth of my jeans. Even the breeze was different—it pushed and tugged at my T-shirt with the gentle hands of angels.

For me the creek was always at its best before sunup, when the juke boxes and the roads were quiet and the gulls had little to squawk about. Nothing existed in those lonely hours but the smells of the waterfront and the purl of the tide against the shore. Dawn brought humanity to the docks, and the change was harsh. Men banged things and cranked engines and rooted around their boats like thieves. On the days I managed to be the first there, the creek seemed to share the tenderest parts of its soul.

I took hold of the Silver Dollar's rigging and swung aboard. It felt heavy underfoot, so sturdy that it hardly reacted to my weight. On deck the mounds of net and ribbon were unfathomable, but through a cabin window I could see bunk beds, neatly made with sheets and blankets. Most cabins I'd seen from the fuel dock were filthy collections of tools and engine parts, but Roy had earned his reputation as the most fastidious skipper on the creek.

More importantly, my captain enjoyed the unqualified re-

spect of his peers. Roy didn't hang around the beer joints anymore, but during his fuel stops at the marina the gossip inside
was always flattering. The common wisdom was that Roy
Pile had taken more shrimp from the Galveston Bay than anyone living or gone.

Roy would tell me that he started shrimping after the war,
when he left the Navy and decided he'd crawled enough Alabama furrows to last three lifetimes. Thank the Lord you're
culling shrimp, he liked to say, because He coulda had you
yanking cotton. When Roy followed a Navy buddy to
Galveston in 1946 there weren't many boats working the bay.
So he decked gulf boats for a couple of years until he found
someone in Maxwell with a bay boat to run.

Them were the glory days, he often said. A man could
throw his net anywhere and pull up five hundred pounds
clean. Now the bay was so heavily fished that the state had
imposed a three hundred pound daily limit, and it took many
boats a full day's work to break it.

But not the Silver Dollar. Roy was uncannily correct about
where to drag, which way to aim, and when to double back.
He could catch shrimp in the same spot for eight straight
days, abandon it for no apparent reason the next, and then
laugh when the radio brought dismal reports about the spot
he'd left behind.

Roy was sixty-one the summer I met him, blessed with
enough guile to make a fortune on the bay but not enough
energy to last the afternoon. The Silver Dollar was the first
boat back to port every day. But we made more money than
most of the fleet in a little more than half the time. Donna had
indeed served me well.

After Roy arrived that first morning, I stood near the transom and watched the dark buildings of Maxwell float by. Our
wake rippled toward shore and urged the boats there into
gentle motion. At the Pier Four, Knuckles stood up on his net
and pulled out what looked like a baby's arm for his morning
constitutional. Tina's Marina was still empty, and I watched
our profile slide along the giant windows of Tony Red's. Roy

leaned on the throttle as we left the channel and I bent my knees deeper for balance. The creek receded behind us, like a forlorn carnival midway.

There was time to drift among the shimmering possibilities beyond our bow. Galveston Bay and the endless oceans that fed it offered everything—soothing rhythms and brazen risks, adventure and inexpressible peace. The warm brine beneath us was connected with the Gulf, the Caribbean, Australia, Peru. Nothing separated us from them but an open prairie of water, the evanescent stuff that trickled so easily through my hands. The wind-blown fullness of life was out there, rolling ceaselessly, waiting for anyone with the will to have it.

I wandered about the boat as if I had just bought it. The swells were deeper out in the bay, but the Silver Dollar plunged through them with the grace of a thoroughbred. I studied the rigging and fussed over the shrimp baskets and plucked remnants of fish from the net. When I wandered back to the cabin Roy was on his stool, cleaning his pipe bowl with a fingernail.

"If you ain't got sense enough to sleep, then listen up," he said. "You watch ever what I do, so I don't gotta show you more than once."

I rubbed my hands together and nodded like a hungry puppy. Roy's eyebrows came to life again.

"I ain't never seen nobody so horny to cull shrimp," he said.

"Well, I am looking forward to it."

"Maybe you're excited about shovel work, too? I got a septic tank that needs laying."

"Thanks, but it just wouldn't be the same."

Roy dipped into a tobacco pouch.

"If cullin' cranks your rotor, you're fixing to be in hog heaven, boy. You're gonna run that deck by yourself, on account of I'm an old man who likes to sit on his fat, lazy ass."

That was the sweetest music I had ever heard.

"So, Donna tells me you're a college boy. What class did you take in that college, anyway?"

"English."

"Shit. Spent all that money just to learn English?"

"Well, yes."

"I'd say they seen you coming, boy."

There was always a gentle edge to Roy's insults, and within minutes we were swapping biographies. He was still married to the woman who came with him from Alabama, a nurse who worked the midnight shift in a rest home. Their daughter was grown, and she had a two-year-old son of her own. Roy said he hadn't invited me in the night before because he was engaged in a "rasslin match" with his grandson.

His plan was to retire in a season or two, and he was in the process of moving his trailer to an acre he'd bought in San Leon.

"Waterfront's an evil place," he said. "A man needs to be as far from sin as he can get before he dies."

*   *   *

Sunup was about ten minutes away when we spotted the squat outline of Redfish Island. Roy pulled back on the throttle and told me to join him on deck. We dumped netting by the armload until the whole rig skimmed along on top of our wake. He moved to the winch and showed me how to hoist the two large wooden doors off the deck. They swung over the stern and spread in the water like papal palms.

Roy took his stool and eased the boat north. For about an hour we followed the imaginary line between markers fifty-seven and fifty-nine on the Houston Ship Channel. Then Roy turned west and walked back on deck to the winch.

I watched him haul in the net and then use a large pulley to hoist it aboard. When he untied the bag and let the catch splash across the deck, it looked as if we'd cut open an elephant. I was suddenly ankle deep in an oozing pile of flesh.

"Nice drag," Roy said. "We can start making two-mile runs."

A slick eel with a dinosaur's head slithered across my boot. Clackety crabs emerged from the gunk, jabbing at the air and attacking each other with their pincers. Some of the shrimp on top flailed like frantic centipedes, but in seconds they were still.

Roy watched me retie the bag and lower the rig into the water. Then he propped a short stool between the catch and a starboard scupper.

He pulled out a few pounds of the catch with a culling rake and began flipping trash fish overboard. They floated belly up on the waves, plump little targets for the sea gulls that yelled at us to work faster. The rake made a squishy sound each time Roy stuck it in the pile.

"There," he said, handing me the rake. "If you're as smart as Donna thinks, that's the last time I'm gonna have to do that."

It was soon apparent why everyone's hands on the waterfront had such an inhuman look. Culling shrimp is like retrieving glass slivers from a bucket of grease. The shrimp, even a dead one, is protected by a needle-sharp horn that juts forward from the head. Cleaning a catch means enduring hundreds of pin pricks, and every prick sizzles with the acidic slime that shrimp secrete.

By eight o'clock, my paws were on fire. Then I broke off a shrimp horn under a thumbnail and made myself heard over the exhaust pipe. Roy and his eyebrows emerged from the cabin.

"Hands gettin' eat up?"

I recited my hottest oaths.

"All you need is something to take your mind off it."

With that he reached down and snatched several hairs from one of my nipples. I covered it with a slimy hand and felt the acid soak in. Roy held the hairs up to his eye and squinted.

"Damn," he said. "You *are* tough for a college boy. Stay with me, son, and you're gonna make a helluva shrimper."

* * *

We were dragging back toward Redfish Island later that morning when a power boat zipped up beside us. The driver was a stocky man with a gold chain nestled in the fur on his chest. His woman was about fifteen years younger, maybe twenty-two years old, with a hot pink bikini and a face nasty enough for a muffler ad. She was tending to four expensive fishing rods in the back.

"Say podnuh," the gold chain said. "How 'bout you give us some shrimp? We're clean outta bait."

Roy emerged slowly from the cabin, his loose shirt flapping around him, and peered down his nose at the bikini.

"Hey, chief. Need me a couple pounds of shrimp. How 'bout it?"

Roy's face moved from the bikini to the driver and back again. His sleepy expression never changed.

"What's it gonna be, man? I ain't got all day."

Roy stared at the girl until she crossed her arms over her breasts. Then he turned and hobbled back to the cabin.

"What the hell's that supposed to mean?"

I shrugged and said, "I guess that was a no."

"Who the fuck do you assholes think you are?"

I squinted into the cabin. Roy was lighting his pipe.

"You're fucking shrimpers, is what you are. Stinking goddamn shrimpers!"

The girl tightened her arms around herself. "Let's just go," she said. "Please."

At that the man punched his throttle and roared away. I turned to Roy and was surprised to see his head swaying slowly with the swells. He had already forgotten who was outside.

Watching thousands of small animals die every day, reaching into prickly goo to cull a catch, finding condescension in the eyes of flabby vacationers…

Shrimpers need a physical and emotional numbness to survive. The numbness had carried Roy Pile though three decades on the bay. And I realized I would need it to have any chance at all.

* * *

As the sun climbed higher I began devising other defenses for the assault on my hands. Spreading the culling piles thinner seemed to help, and I lifted clumps of shrimp by their tangled whiskers when I could. My fingers still felt as stiff as Knuckles', but at least the swelling brought on the welcome numbness—the numbness of a shrimper.

Between catches I spent a lot of time on the bow, savoring the water and the grace of the gulls. Those were the best moments, the moments I had run away from the world to find. There was nothing to accomplish here, no mountains to scale. Life was good for the living of it. On the bay I was already capable enough, worthy enough, happy enough, to be the human being that I was.

But the girl was stolen.

How fitting that Donna, who had done so much to bring me into this world, was now the only thing keeping me from it. Deciding what to do about Sharlene was to decide what to do about me.

Roy headed back for the docks just after one o'clock. On our way home I picked the net cleaner than it had probably been in years and arranged the deck equipment even more impressively than Roy had left it. He wandered back to check on things and couldn't fight the urge to smile.

"Not bad, college." He lifted a few folds of net and shook his head. "Not bad at all. Sam, how about taking the wheel awhile?"

I settled onto the stool and grasped the wooden spokes the way a priest takes a ciborium. The Silver Dollar swung slow but sure where I aimed her, plunging deep into the mounds of water in our way. Up ahead the drawbridge arched over our hamlet of white and silver boxes, its steel girders glinting in the sun.

The girl was stolen. She was being raised by a barmaid—and by a shrimper capable of sudden violence. And somewhere on the outside, away from the waterfront, a young

woman was probably desperate, praying for help from someone like me.

But the engine was roaring, the wind was blowing, and
our boat was beating across the bay. I closed my eyes to the
sunshine and let my head sway slowly with the swells.

*   *   *

Donna was rinsing the fuel dock when she caught sight of
us. She raised a tentative hand and strained to read my face.
Something called her inside before we could motor close, and
I found myself feeling relieved.

From my first day on the waterfront I had looked forward
to the moment when I could stride into the marina with my
boots on. But the sight of Donna made me almost sick with
dread. Would she ever tell me about the girl? If she didn't,
would I ever ask?

By the time I returned to Tina's Marina, I had decided to
slink upstairs. There was too much at stake now—my sanity,
my life—and something told me I could never set foot in the
bar until I was sure I'd still be a shrimper when I walked out
again.

So I showered, threw open the window, and let the breeze
dry me as I drifted into fitful sleep. There were images of the
bay then, and of Roy, the catch, Donna...Sharlene. Later I felt
a weight on the bed, and I woke to find Donna, undressed
and slightly sweaty, sitting beside me. She forced an anemic
smile, and both of us knew we were in danger.

"Hey," she said hoarsely. "I expected to see you in the bar.
How'd you like it out there, Sam?"

Before I could speak she blurted, "I know what Bunny told
you last night."

I took a long, careful breath.

"I got a friend who works over there. Said she heard the
whole thing."

I watched the beautiful dangle of Donna's breasts as she
crawled over to straddle my shins. She ran her hands slowly

up my legs and said, "I think we need to have us a talk, Sam."

"A *talk*, huh?" I was torn between urges to slap her face and to draw it down onto me. "Funny, we didn't *talk* yesterday, or the day before, or ever since the first time we *talked*."

"I mean it, Sam." She began to stroke me. "We need to talk—you and me and Fletcher—about what Bunny told you."

Before I realized it I had shoved her aside and jumped out of bed. "Get out," I said. "I'm not interested in a bribery fuck."

Donna sank onto her ankles, her legs spread indelicately, and looked out the window.

"Is that what you think?"

I was too angry to answer.

"We need to talk, Sam, yes. But that's got nothing to do with this."

"Well, what is this, then? Leo didn't show up, maybe?"

Donna sighed heavily and leaned against the wall. "I knew we shoulda never done it. I told you it would mess things up between us."

"Shit, who's messing up now? I didn't invite you up here. No, all of a sudden you just can't live without me. And my finding out about Sharlene is just a coincidence."

"Sam, please. Whatever else you think about me, whatever you decide, you've got to believe this. I'm here because I want to be."

"Then why..." I felt myself weaken. "...why has it taken until now?"

Donna climbed off the bed and took a beer from the icebox.

"I was afraid for you, Sam."

"Afraid for me?"

"Scared of what might happen to you if you got mixed up in this." She took a slow drink, then pressed the can against her forehead. "But now, after what Bunny did, it's too late for that."

I felt my heart sink. Things were moving too fast. I was

sliding, sliding deep into something I wanted no part of, something ugly.

I asked for the beer and tilted it mechanically. But I couldn't taste it, and I felt some of it roll down my chest.

Donna guided me to the foot of the bed and knelt before me. I heard her say something about Fletcher and Sharlene and a restaurant far from the water. I heard her say that after today I would finally understand everything.

And then, arching my back, my eyes fixed on the gray-green chop of the bay, I heard myself think: *Make me believe you, Donna. Please, make me believe...*

Eleven

Fletcher's boat had already sunk to the cabin ports when Donna reached the dock. It was over, everything gone. His beloved boat, her bar, their livelihood, the trailer, every last hope of recapturing the magic—gone.

Donna sat on the dock and stared. She felt herself drifting into the darkness over the boat, above Fletcher's domain, over the place she was never supposed to go. The boat was so small and silent under the water, so dead. Everything was over and done, every single thing.

She pulled her knees in close and rocked slowly in the breeze. *Life will be miserable enough in the morning,* she thought. *Just enjoy this while you can...*

* * *

Donna had told me, during one of our private afternoons at Tina's, that the night Fletcher's boat sank was the best night of her life.

She made me swear never to tell him that. And until Bunny blurted the story about Sharlene, I thought I was in on Donna's most sensitive secret. It shed so much light on the how and why of Fletcher's fall from grace. And Donna's account of the sinking had given me the closest glimpse yet into her enshrouded heart.

From her very first day on the boat, Donna remembered,

her presence had changed everything. Until then Fletcher always worked alone, and no woman had even set foot on his deck before. Now Donna was there, doing the work he couldn't do, crowding into the solitude that had renewed him every time he left the land. Nothing would ever be the same.

"The first day was probably the worst day in both our lives," Donna told me. "Fletcher was hung over as hell. I never saw him drunk, before or since, the way he was drunk the night before we left."

He was still in a cast, and he almost killed himself getting on the boat. But he swatted away Donna's hand every time she tried to help. The cabin stool couldn't hold him and he had to stand all day, trying to ignore the pain in his leg and in his head.

Fletcher kept his instructions terse and incomplete. But Donna soon mastered the craft anyway, standing steadily on the deck and flicking hair from her eyes as if she'd been born to the work. She didn't even complain about her hands.

Other shrimpers noticed Fletcher's boat on the water and tried to raise him on the radio. He ignored their calls but heard the banter about what had gotten into ol' Fletch—and how nice it must be to have a perfumed deck hand on the back of your boat.

Everything was different. When she finished culling a load, Donna would come into the cabin humming, flirting, filling the place up so a man couldn't think. He knew she meant well, but hell, it just wasn't right.

Donna was changing, too. First she stopped worrying about her fingernails. It was a waste of time, and long nails only got in the way. Then she quit getting her hair fixed, because the wind just blew it out. Makeup became a burden, too: It was silly to get fixed up for a bunch of crabs.

But Donna loved the water. The bright sky reminded her of good times with her father. Sometimes she caught herself smiling at the back of Fletcher's head. He'd lost a lot of himself, just as her father had, but Donna once again was finding more of herself in the process. He needed her, and she was coming through.

If she loved the sun, it seemed eager to return the sentiment. Her face and arms took on a rich brown hue, and as she worked she could feel the blood move soothingly through her muscles. She never wore a hat or a visor—not even sunglasses. They got in the way of summer and kept the heat from opening her up, making her strong and new.

But everything was different. Fletcher started bringing a six-pack along in the morning. His old knack for finding busy shrimp beds seemed to be deserting him. He never helped with the culling, even when he started moving well enough to do it. All he ever did was stare straight ahead, listening to the radio squelch, without uttering a sound.

His weight continued to fall. He shaved and bathed less often. His dentures stayed on the dresser for days at a time. As the summer wore on he began to develop a humble stoop. Fletcher was getting old.

And he was making mistakes, stupid ones, mistakes that never would have happened before. One day he wrapped the net around a submerged wreck near the power plant, a hazard that had been there for decades and was known to every shrimper with a week's experience.

That mishap cost Donna and Fletcher their net, the doors, most of their cable and four days of refitting. There was nothing Donna could do when Fletcher, incensed, cut the rig free with a hacksaw and roared away without a word.

"On the way home," Donna told me, "I kept thinking how he gave up so easy. He just quit without a fight, the same way Daddy always did. It broke my heart to see it. I remember thinking, `Why is it that the vile men get ahead and the good men always fail?'"

Weeks passed with an empty monotony, and Donna began seeing an older, tighter face in the mirror. Fletcher was drunk every day by noon and asleep before sundown. They both found reasons to avoid the beer joints over which they had once reigned. Too many memories, too many unhappy comparisons. There would be whispers about how the sun aged a woman, how having a woman aboard really took it out of a man. Donna and Fletcher never talked about it, because to even think those things was to admit they were true.

One evening Fletcher, dulled by Lone Star, barreled into the channel and brushed heavily against a boat at the Captain Borneo. The other skipper was knocked off his feet in the collision, and he demanded a piece of the damn fool who could have killed him and his boat. Fletcher emerged from his cabin with blazing eyes. That alone would have ended the controversy only months before, but everything was different now. Fletcher was a skinny old man who drank beer all day to forget he was a skinny old man who drank beer.

"He snapped," Donna remembered. "I begged him to stay in the cabin and let the thing blow over, but that was just oil on the fire. Fletcher climbed up on the tramsom and told the guy if he didn't like the way he ran his boat, he was gonna take and shove a boot up his ass."

The other captain started for Fletcher. Donna jumped into the cabin and hit the throttle. The lurch threw Fletcher overboard and left him hanging by his fingers from the other man's boat, submerged to his belt in the creek. As Donna stared back in horror, she let the boat ram an empty dock a few yards away.

The commotion drew crowds on both sides of the creek, and there was scattered applause when the skipper and his deck hand pulled Fletcher aboard. The fight was over, with neither man in a position to confront the other any longer.

Donna backed up slowly. The other captain slapped Fletcher on the butt when he jumped aboard, the way a coach comforts a Little Leaguer after a strikeout. Donna moved silently out of Fletcher's way. Apologizing would have made it worse. She watched a puddle form around him as he pulled away from the dock and wandered the bay until everyone was surely gone. Donna and Fletcher didn't speak to one another for days.

Donna's collision had another lasting effect. It was soon

apparent that the bilge pump was cycling more often, evidence that the dock had loosened a board or punctured the hull below the waterline. Fletcher and Donna had neither the money nor the time for a mid-season haul out. But every morning her first waking thought was of the pump. Had it held out? Was it going to last the summer? Wasn't it starting to sound a little rough?

Fletcher greeted the questions at first with apathy and then with growing annoyance. He was pulling himself farther and farther away from her, from the boat, from everything except his beer. It became Donna's practice to check the pump every night after sundown. The reassurance helped her sleep, and the short drive to the dock gave her a few precious minutes alone. If Fletcher hadn't been trying so hard to throw himself away, it would have been him making the checks. But Fletcher was lost, and Donna knew it was up to her to be sure.

She fretted over the pump for weeks before Fletcher finally agreed to buy a backup. He left for Texas City one afternoon around four. He and the pump were due back in a couple of hours, but by ten o'clock there hadn't been a word. If he'd fallen into trouble, Donna would have heard by then. No, he was drunk somewhere, maybe with the pump and maybe not. All he had for certain was the car.

"I was so mad I could hardly see," Donna said. "I started walking to the marina to check on the boat. The pump was ready to go out any minute, but did he give a shit? No, it was me out there walking, hoping I didn't have to get the fire department to pump it out before it sank."

Donna was halfway to the marina when two headlights drew up from behind. It was Mickie, one of her old barmaids at the beer joint. Come on, Mickie was saying, let's get us a couple of cold ones for old time's sake. Donna started to say no, that the pump was on its last legs, that the boat could drop to the mud in the time it took to empty two beers. But she heard herself say sure, by God, that sounds like a winner to me.

They went to Tina's, and the place was filled with friends

she hadn't seen in months. She found herself dancing and laughing and flirting as if the old days had never ended. Everyone was nicer to her than they had ever been. Donna told herself it wasn't sympathy she saw in their faces, but respect, affection, even love.

"Mickie got lucky and was long gone when the last call went out," Donna said. "I decided to go sleep on the boat. I figured it would serve Fletcher right to come back and find the house empty—and me snoring up a storm on his precious vessel."

But Fletcher's boat had already sunk to the cabin ports when Donna reached the dock. It was over, everything gone. His beloved boat, her bar, their livelihood, the trailer, every last hope of recapturing the magic—gone.

And when she sat on the dock and pulled her knees in close, Donna floated out into the night, the best night of her life, as light and as free as a seagull on the breeze.

Twelve

As she left my room, Donna said she'd bring Fletcher and Sharlene to the marina around seven that night. That gave me some time to myself, and there was something I had to do before I saw her again.

I drove from bar to bar, on both sides of the creek, until finally I found it: the giant black pickup that led me to Bunny. I was staring at the tailgate, trying to collect myself, when her boyfriend emerged from the bar and saw me.

"Whatcha doin' out here?" he said gaily. "Looks like you just seen a ghost or something."

I mumbled that I was fine.

"I'm on a cigarette run, 'cause they're out of Bunny's brand. Anything I can get ya?"

"No thanks. Guess I'll just go in and have a beer."

"Good deal. Keep Bunny company for me, OK?"

I watched the wind play with the shell dust as he drove away. Then I heard Bunny's voice through the screen door.

"Well, look who's here," she said. "Damned if it ain't Joe College."

I stepped inside and slumped onto the stool next to hers. We looked at one another in the mirror behind the bar.

"I know why you're here," she said. "But it ain't gonna do you no good."

"I want to know the truth, Bunny. The whole story."

"Forget it. I told you the first day I saw you that I don't

want no knives shoved down my throat."

I motioned for a beer and bought another setup for Bunny.

"I'm having dinner with her," I said. "Fletcher, Sharlene...we're all going somewhere inland. She says she's going to tell me everything."

"Yeah, sure," Bunny muttered. "And you're probably going to believe it."

"Then why don't you set me straight? Is she kidnapped, or isn't she? What does `stolen' mean? Do her parents—"

"Stop it, Sam. And keep your damn voice down." Bunny leaned toward me, glancing around the room. "I told you I ain't getting involved, and that's that."

"Please, Bunny, I'm begging you."

"Ha!" She straightened herself and poured bourbon over her fresh ice. "Why should I stick my neck out for you, Sam? I tried to help you twice already, and all I got both times was a mouthful of shit. No...you made your own bed, so now you can just sleep in it."

"We're talking about a little girl," I said. "This isn't about me."

"The hell it ain't! That's exactly what this is about—and you know it."

Bunny reached instinctively for her empty cigarette pack, then wadded it and threw it at my reflection.

"You're on your own now, buddy boy. And you wanna know what I think? I think you're in way over your fucking head."

*   *   *

Sharlene squirmed out of Fletcher's arms when she realized I would be driving us to dinner. She was too young to care about food, but old enough to see the prospect of adventure in an unfamiliar car. She hopped in place by the door while I dug out my keys.

"Better open it before she goes crazy," Donna said. "Let's try to keep the dress clean for five minutes anyway."

Sharlene's tan was set off by a bright yellow sundress and white sandals. Her hair, still wet from a bath, was combed straight back like a silent film siren's. The tiny pearls in her ears seemed almost to glisten in the sun.

When I swung open the door, Sharlene marveled at the terrain of unexplored upholstery. Fletcher limped into the back seat like a playmate, folding up his long legs and helping her arrange herself beside him. There was no doubting his devotion to the girl—he and Donna didn't even discuss who would join me in front.

Fletcher was a different man when he had a chance to bask in Sharlene's glow. His chin rested a few notches higher around her, and he seemed to regard the world with added confidence. Donna still wore the vocal cords in the family, but Fletcher was more a participant and less a spectator in the company of his little prize.

Donna directed me south to Grady's, a small place in San Leon specializing in chicken fried steak. On the way, she stretched her arm out the window and watched the wind wash over it.

It occurred to me that Donna had come full circle in her years on the waterfront, transformed from an entrepreneur to a cowering mistress to a resilient woman in control of herself and two others. When Fletcher's boat went down and she took the marina job to support them, the transformation was complete.

Fletcher appeared relaxed in the rear-view mirror, now and again following a weed as it whizzed by. Donna hadn't told him what this was about, and he was no more aware of his destiny than Sharlene was.

"Two! Two!"

She was up on her knees now, pointing to a pair of sunglasses on the dashboard. I passed them back, and Fletcher slipped them gently onto her nose.

"Hey," I said. "Who's the stranger with the shades?"

Sharlene crawled over Fletcher to find herself in the mirror. She rested her chin on my shoulder and smiled at both of us. Donna brought her arm in from the warm air, then turned to Fletcher.

"Bet you're wondering what's the deal," she said.

Fletcher nodded expectantly.

"Bunny told Sam how we got a hold of you-know-who."

Fletcher's grin evaporated. He looked at me as if I were a constable assigned to take the girl away.

"Don't worry," Donna said. "I told Sam we'd bring him up to speed on everything."

Fletcher was not assured. He folded his hands in his lap, as he did the first day I saw him in the marina. I thought of a stricken schoolboy waiting for the principal to get his father on the phone.

"Wait a minute," I said. "This little conference was Donna's idea, so don't think I'm prying."

Donna and Fletcher exchanged glances.

"Fletch don't mind," she finally said. "Ain't nothing he could do about it, even if he did."

The pronouncement seemed to soothe him, and he drifted back out among the weeds.

*   *   *

Grady's was a converted summer house with ceiling fans, small rooms, and a back yard playground to attract the family trade. It was the place where Donna and Fletcher had gone for refuge during their glory days.

Grady, a short man with a red toupee, seemed stunned by his old customers' new incarnations.

"My God," he whispered. "It's—it's been forever, hasn't it?"

The surroundings seemed to carry Donna back in time. She sighed happily and grabbed Fletcher's elbow with both hands. But the touch of his withered arm seemed to douse the fantasy.

"Yeah," she finally said. "Last time we were here...that was a helluva lot of teeth ago."

The remark put Grady in visible pain. Then he noticed Sharlene among the folds of Fletcher's pants.

"New addition to the family?"

"That's our Sharlene," Donna said, more for my benefit than Grady's. "She's our little girl." Then she nudged Fletcher. "Bet you thought ol' Big Boy didn't have it in him."

Fletcher seemed to enjoy the joke, but Grady was losing his breath.

"No ma'am, no. If anybody had it in him, it was Fletcher Quinn."

Grady's use of the past tense lingered in the air like sulfur. He hurried to change the subject.

"I still remember your favorite table," he said. "It's going to be just like the old days."

We came to a room with a broad view of the oaks and ivy in the yard. Sharlene pressed her nose to the window and took special interest in the sand pits around the horseshoe stakes. When we sat, Grady bent at the waist and looked toward Fletcher.

"The usual?"

"Sure," Donna said. "Three times, and a hot dog for the squirt."

Grady adjusted Sharlene's kiddie chair.

"And what would you like to drink, young lady?"

"Two!"

"That means Coke," Donna said.

Grady took our beer order and headed for the kitchen looking vaguely depressed. Donna sighed and propped her chin on her palms. She had let her hair down after the car ride, and it tumbled nicely around her beautiful face.

"We had us a lot of good times here," she said to no one in particular. "Seems like a hundred years ago."

Fletcher's attention never left Sharlene, who was already impatient with her chair. He reached over to brush a hair from her face and grinned when she squirmed away. Soon Sharlene was at the window again, pointing to the sandboxes and whimpering to Fletcher.

"Hold your horses," Donna said. "You can go out in a while, but first we gotta eat."

Sharlene stomped a foot, then abruptly lowered herself to the hardwood floor, face down, like a nun taking her vows. Donna and Fletcher seemed not to notice.

Grady appeared with our drinks and three heaping salads. Fletcher eyed his plate squeamishly after Grady left.

"Something wrong?" I said.

Donna leaned toward me and lowered her voice. "It's fine, Sam. But the only thing about lettuce is, you gotta have the teeth for it."

Fletcher grinned and blew a shot of air into his beer can.

"Steak, we can gum to death," Donna explained. "This stuff might as well be corn on the cob for all the good it's gonna do us."

Sharlene hadn't budged from the floor. Donna saw me watching her.

"That's the way she pouts, Sam. She'd stay there a week if she could remember how come she got mad."

I reached down to turn her over, and she was stiff as a corpse. Only the slightest flutter of her eyelids told me she was still alive.

"Two?" I said.

Sharlene stifled a smile and rolled back onto her stomach.

"She'll get up when she smells her weenie," Donna said. "Don't make a fuss when she does."

Dinner came, and Sharlene quietly took her chair as if nothing had happened. Fletcher cut her food into manageable chunks, which she arranged in a circle.

The sight of Donna and Fletcher grappling with steak was a special treat. With every bite their lower jaws seemed to disappear into their skulls. Donna caught me spying.

"Pretty slick, ain't it? Just remember, boy, this could be you someday."

Donna's good mood didn't jibe with our purpose here. She wasn't drunk—she was still on her first beer when Fletcher and I ordered our third—but she seemed almost giddy.

Maybe it was the relief that comes when that which is dreaded finally arrives. Or maybe she was confident her story would win me.

Fletcher was the first to push his plate away, and he immediately began losing a battle with his eyelids. Sharlene's attention was on the yard again, and I found myself wondering if Donna had forgotten why we were here.

"Hey, kiddo, wanna play outside?"

Donna hadn't finished the sentence before Sharlene was pulling on Fletcher's arm. He found his feet and dutifully followed her from the room. Outside, Sharlene bounded to one of the sand boxes while Fletcher sat heavily on a bench.

"Tell me," Donna said, "what would you do if you found out someone had taken someone else's kid?"

Hearing it phrased it so bluntly left me at a loss.

"You know what I mean, Sam. What if you found out, and you knew where the kid was?"

I was beginning to resent this. Donna was the accused, and I was the one squirming.

"I've got a better idea, Donna. Just say what you came here to say."

She looped her hair behind her ears and watched me so intently I had to look outside. Sharlene was burying her legs in one of the sand pits. Gravity had taken command of Fletcher's chin.

"Sharlene thinks the world of you, Sam. Know what she was doing when I picked her up today? Reading a book, or anyway, pretending she was. It was a regular book with print, no pictures. And there she was, licking her finger, turning the pages one at a time.

"I know she didn't pick that up from Fletch or me. She was imitating you, Sam, doing what she's seen you do out on the patio."

Sharlene looked up from the sandbox and waved.

"Sam, I wonder if you've ever noticed the way people do things to punish themselves. Like maybe they figure if they suffer enough, do things they don't want to do, then they'll

get right with the Lord or something. You ever know anybody like that?"

I shrugged and kept my eyes on the girl.

"Sharlene's momma was one of those. She was a barmaid
of mine. Got herself pregnant—God knows who with—and
decided the thing to do was to keep the baby.

"Only she didn't want no baby. She didn't want nothing,
except maybe her next beer or her next fella. But all of a sudden she got it in her mind that she'd led a sinner's life, and
keeping the baby was gonna be her way to straighten out.

"Pretty soon after she had Sharlene, all that repent stuff
went out the window. The straight and narrow wasn't as fun as
she thought it was gonna be. And there she was, stuck with a
little kid that needed feeding and diapering and what-all else.

"That's when she started asking me if I wanted her little
girl."

Grady came by with the coffee pot. Donna fidgeted until
he left.

"Fletcher...well, me and Fletcher didn't want no part of no
baby. He'd just left two children of his own and besides, we
didn't have no place for it, living behind the bar the way we
was.

"But when we got the trailer, I started thinking about it
some. She was such a cute little thing, and she wasn't getting
raised worth a damn.

"Sharlene's momma would give her whiskey to make her
sleep, and then leave her alone in the house all night. And she
kept after us, telling us we were the best people she could
think of to raise her.

"But then I lost the bar, and we wound up working the
boat all day just to stay even."

Donna looked out into the yard and wrestled with a dozen
emotions. When she finally turned back to me I couldn't believe it—her eyes were brimming with tears.

"You've probably wondered where this came from." She
ran a thumb along the shiny scar under her jaw. "It was
Fletcher."

My head snapped to the passive pile of bones outside.

"It happened the night the boat sank."

The night the boat sank...Donna had called it the best night of her life.

"Jesus, how could you stay with him after he did that?"

"You gotta remember," she said softly, "that man went from the top of the world to the bottom in just a few months. When he broke his hip and our whole life went to shit...all of a sudden he wasn't a strong man no more. Fletcher never had nothing besides that.

"Then the next thing he knows, he's got a woman on his boat, and she's acting like she's the boss half the time. And then the grand finale—the boat sinks."

I realized Donna had never finished the story about that night. It couldn't have ended with her sitting on the dock. Fletcher, inevitably, found out about it...

* * *

"He finally came back from Texas City about three in the morning with a head full of liquor," Donna said. "The house was empty, and he knew before he got to the marina that there was big trouble. The rigging on the boat was low, way too low.

"Fletcher drove up expecting a crowd of people trying to save it. But all he saw was me, sitting there on the dock in front of his pride and joy. He got out of the car and came at me like an animal.

"'Hey!' he says, 'Getting you a good night's sleep? Hope you didn't hurt yourself trying to save the boat!' Next thing I know he's standing over me, kicking me, slapping me all over. He's got a hold of his whiskey bottle, and he's hitting me with it, too. Sure enough, it broke in half and cut my face wide open."

Donna caught herself when she saw the effect this was having on me.

"But listen, Sam. When Fletcher seen what he done, he

slumped down on the ground and cried like he'd just killed his mother. It broke him, broke him all the way—he'd lost himself for good. Me, I was gonna recover, but Fletcher...we both knew he was gone."

Donna's face was burning and shiny with blood, but she found herself kneeling next to Fletcher, stroking him, trying to caress away his pain. He was so weak, so helpless...as lost as her father had ever been.

"Something wouldn't let me leave him, Sam. Sometimes all you can see is how much you've hurt someone. After all, he got ruined in the first place trying to help me, and I paid him back by putting a hole in his boat."

Donna reached past her coffee for the beer, then suddenly pushed it away. "Hell, that wasn't all of it. Part of me was glad to see him broke down. He deserved that and worse, after everything he'd done to me.

"But I didn't want to go, Sam. For the first time I was free to get up and walk away, but I didn't want to go."

That terrible night on the dock only speeded the inevitable. Fletcher's boat wasn't properly insured, he had no money to fix it, and the bank refused to help. He finally sold it for a fraction of its worth. Donna took her job in the marina, and Fletcher started running a beat-up boat that even Knuckles had refused.

Before summer's end they had lost the mobile home and moved to a one-room apartment miles from the bay. Donna was treading water, no longer enraptured with Fletcher but not miserable enough to abandon him.

She recited the story in a detached monotone, never pausing over a word or considering which tributary of the past to follow next. I knew she wasn't in the habit of talking about these things, yet it sounded so facile, almost rehearsed. Donna hadn't even come to Sharlene yet, but something in my stomach was telling me I couldn't believe her.

Out in the yard, Sharlene was involved in an intrigue near Fletcher's feet. Moving carefully so she wouldn't wake him, she raised a yo-yo proudly from the grass. I couldn't bring myself to smile. Donna knew she was losing me.

"I was working evenings when it happened," she said. "One night I closed up the marina and went out to the car. And there she was, Sharlene, locked inside and sound asleep on the front seat. She just a tiny thing, lying there with her pierced ears and her white hair like some kind of baby princess.

"Her momma left a note on the windshield. She must have gone crazy or something. She said it kept going over and over in her mind that Sharlene would be better off dead than with her. Said she hadn't fed her in two days and just couldn't bring herself to do it no more.

"Then this voice or this vision or something told her she ought to leave the baby with me and just get the hell off the waterfront. She figured I'd do right by Sharlene then, on account of I wasn't tied up with the boat no more.

"I didn't know what to do. I got her some food and took here home, and after a while I laid her down on the bed next to Fletch. He woke up and saw that baby, sleeping so peaceful and sweet next to him, and tears just started pouring out of him."

For a moment, Donna picked at the tablecloth. "He needed her, Sam. He needed her bad. Fletcher didn't have nothing. Sharlene was the only one in the world who didn't know he had any reason to be ashamed. So I decided right there—all right, we're gonna raise us a little girl."

I felt a warm swell of relief—and then remembered Bunny.

"But it doesn't add up," I said. "I don't see how Bunny gets a stolen baby out of that."

"Let me finish, Sam." Donna's voice was quavering. I wasn't the only one whose future was riding on this conversation.

"At first, things went along fine," she said. "No problems, everything smooth. You can see for yourself how Fletcher and Sharlene get along. She saved his life.

"Then—it was about six months ago—Sharlene's momma came back. She'd hooked up with some dragster, I don't know, a funny-car racer, something. He went all over the country to the different tracks. They had some money, and she decided she wanted her baby back.

"They traced me down to the apartment one morning. I was working nights back then. Fletcher was out on the water, and there I was, standing in front of two people who wanted me to hand over their baby.

"What else could I do? I didn't want to give her up, and I knew it would tear the heart out of Fletcher. But I had no place holding onto a baby that wasn't mine, especially with her momma right there asking for her back. The man seemed nice enough. And besides, she could have filed charges on me.

"Alright, I told them, alright. If it means that much to you, I won't stand in the way. All I asked was that they didn't go nowhere until Fletcher had a chance to see her. I didn't want him to come home and just find her gone.

"Well, Sharlene's momma didn't care for that much. But the fella—he was a pretty nice guy, really—he agreed to it. They even came over for a few beers at the marina when I started my shift. I left a note at home for Fletcher and said we'd wait for him.

"I really didn't know how it was gonna affect him. I mean, I knew it would make him sick, but I didn't know what he'd do about it. I guess I really figured he wouldn't come to the marina at all, that he'd just go out somewhere and get drunk. I kinda talked them into staying so I could at least see Sharlene awhile longer."

Donna's face began to brighten.

"Well, Fletcher showed up, alright—carrying this piece of stainless steel pipe. He said nobody was taking his baby girl, least of all a slut who could lock her in a car and run off. He said he didn't care if he went straight to the electric chair, he was gonna swing that pipe and keep swinging it until he got hold of the baby. And then he was going to kill anybody who ever tried to get her back.

"The race car driver got real spooked. He kinda handed

Sharlene over and backed out the door. I couldn't believe it. Fletcher had scared the shit out of the guy! Sharlene's momma went running after him, but he drove off without her and never came back.

"Well, you might have figured it. She didn't have no use for no baby then. She left that night and hasn't shown her face since. Anyway, that's how Bunny got kidnapping out of the deal. I guess we did steal Sharlene, in a way. But her momma sure ain't filed no charges."

I was leaning forward when Donna finished, and I felt myself begin to deflate. The story was so wild it just might have been true—and so wild it probably wasn't.

"What you thinking, Sam?"

I watched Sharlene pull up a handful of grass and then arrange it, blade by blade, in Fletcher's hair.

"I don't know what to think. I guess I wouldn't have thought Fletcher had it in him."

Donna considered that for a moment.

"People will surprise you sometimes. What do they call it? Rising to the occasion?"

Yes, I said. Yes. They call it rising to the occasion.

Thirteen

No one was on the patio when we pulled into Tina's, so Donna suggested we cap the evening with a beer under the stars.

She seemed pleased that Fletcher and Sharlene couldn't be roused in the back seat. When I came outside carrying two sweaty cans, Donna was sitting on the edge of the dock, watching the distant lights of a tanker headed south to the gulf.

She took a long, slow drink and said, "You don't know what you're going to do, do you Sam?"

My awkward silence proved she was right.

"Well, there's something else to consider, you know. And that's you."

I felt a quick tingle. Was Donna prepared at last to tell me where the two of us really stood?

"Sam, I know how much all this means to you—the docks, the bay, the boats, everything. But the truth is, if you go outside the waterfront with this...well, you'll be through here."

I glanced toward the bridge so Donna wouldn't see how much that hurt.

"It wouldn't be me doing it, Sam. But word would get around what you done. People on the creek don't take kindly to—"

"Outsiders," I snapped. "Outsiders and anybody who rubs up against one."

"Sam, it seems like I'm hitting below the belt. But it's for your sake as much as anything."

"Yeah, I'm sure."

It wasn't the blatant manipulation that stung so much. It wasn't even the hint that self-interest would turn me away from doing what was right. What hit hardest at that moment was the idea I had been pegged again. And I didn't take it well.

"Alright, Donna, since we're trading rabbit punches, let me give you some friendly advice. Keep screwing three guys—or however many it is—and it's just a matter of time before one of them tries to kill another one, if he doesn't go after you first."

Donna set down her beer deliberately and looked back to the bay.

"For your information," she said, her voice unsteady, "I ain't fucking no three men."

"Come on, Donna, I can count. My audit shows Fletcher, Leo and who else? Oh, yes. Young shit-for-brains here wins the bronze."

"You don't understand, Sam."

"Oh, so there are more than three."

"No."

"How many? Five? Six?"

"Shut up."

"Are we talking double figures here?"

"Listen, dammit, Fletcher don't fuck!"

Donna had shouted at such a volume that the creek suddenly sounded dead. We looked at each other queasily and then held our breaths as we turned toward the car. Fletcher was still lost in a deep, gape-mouthed slumber.

"He's been out of it since the accident, Sam. I don't know whether he can't do it because of what's happened to him—or whether he let everything happen to him because he can't do it."

"I'm sorry," I said sickly. "I was lashing out—it's none of my—"

"And Leo, well, Leo's a good guy. And he's very kind to me. Fletcher would shit if he knew how much of what little we have comes from Leo.

"I mean, he has to know there's somebody else. He never says nothing about it. But I'm sure he wouldn't expect me to go all this time without...well..."

Donna picked up her beer and emptied it. I offered her a sip of mine, but she reached for my hand.

"Listen, Sam, I'm gonna level with you. What I'd really like is for things to stay just like they are. Tomorrow, or next month maybe—I don't know—maybe then it'll be time for something else. But things have been pretty decent lately, and I don't want to go messing it up with changes or fancy new plans."

"Right," I said, trying to smile. "We know what plans and dreams did to your mother."

"That's one reason I was afraid to get tangled up with you. With you, it's almost like my momma's alive again, and that's scary.

"Listen, Sam. Bunny didn't do you no favors by drawing you into my shit, and I'm sorry for it. I should have done a better job of staying away from you, too, and I'm sorry for that."

I tightened my grip on her hand. "Now it's you who doesn't understand. Knowing you...these last weeks have been the most wonderful time of my life. I want us to—"

"Hush," she said softly. "If something's good, you should leave it alone. A young man shouldn't be taking on a load like me and Sharlene."

"But Donna, I've been thinking...and then this afternoon, when we were upstairs, I knew..." She shook her head slightly, but I went on. "There's nothing, Donna, nothing in the world I want more than you."

"Today, maybe. Right now. But take it from me, the whole thing would fall apart."

"I can't believe that."

"Well, I can. Let's just enjoy what we've got for as long as we enjoy it. And let's wipe every bit of trouble from our minds."

She leaned toward me. I felt her soft lips touch mine. And then I helped her wake Sharlene and Fletcher.

They waved groggy goodbyes as Donna steered her car westward, away from me and the murky waterfront, inland toward their home.

*   *   *

Late that night when the marina closed, I wandered down the creek to the Silver Dollar. Summer still hadn't unleashed its angriest heat, but the air was relentlessly close. I peeled off my shirt and felt my skin open up in the darkness.

For the first time in my life, a lifetime of impotent silence, I was beginning to make the faint sounds of a human being. This place, this chance, this woman...if I turned back now I was lost. I could never survive on the bay—or even be permitted to—unless I committed to it whole.

If Donna's story was a lie, then hiding Sharlene would keep an innocent mother from her child. There was ample reason to doubt her, but who appointed me to find out? There were people whose job it was to decide, people trained to find out, to make the right choice.

But they were on the outside, the *outside*, the black void into which I would be flung if I tried to bring them here.

And I knew what I would do. I knew, because there comes a time in a miserable fool's life when he can only find himself by putting himself somewhere.

Fourteen

We were floating near the ship channel one warm night, tied to another boat and waiting for the sun. Roy and I were mending the net. The other boat's captain, a young but waterwise man with a beard that reached his biceps, was crowing about his latest run-in with the game wardens.

"Good thing them bastards ain't got sniffin' dawgs," he said. "Dawg woulda had my ass cold."

Roy worked the threader with an indulgent smile. Garland was a pretty good shrimper, but not a smart one. He was too full of himself to respect the quiet of the night.

"Fuckin' warden, he's down on his hands and knees—it's all I can do to keep my boot out his ass. He's got his nose six inches from the damn shrimp. Fucker just shakes his head and says, `I know you got 'em somewheres, Garland, but you can fuck me naked if I know where they are.'

"I felt like telling the thief to grab some Vasoline 'cause he was standing on nine hundred pounds of illegal shrimp."

Roy kept sewing. He'd heard so much bullshit in his years on the bay that it hardly sank in anymore. Garland unzipped his jeans and pissed off the stern.

"How they expect us to live on three hundred pounds a day, I'll never know. Not with what they're paying at the fish house. A man might as well tie it up and leave it if he's gonna obey the damn law. Bites my ass."

Roy didn't care much for butt-kicking bluster, but he

wasn't smug about it. If it made a man feel good to fling some shit, Roy wasn't going to stop him.

Garland sat on a bucket and ran a knife under his finger-nails, realizing at last that no one else had spoken in fifteen minutes. *Fuck 'em if they don't wanna talk,* he was telling him-self. *I got better things to do than entertain their ass.*

I had been with Roy more than a month—forty-two con-secutive days to be exact. He was a religious man, but he didn't believe in resting on the Sabbath if the shrimp didn't.

So we met wordlessly in the dark every morning and headed east toward the brightening sky. Everything on the Silver Dollar radiated the success of the harvest, the struggle of muscle against weight, the nervous contest between hunter and prey.

And I was there, working on it, succeeding on it, acting on the first real decision I had made about my life. The mere act of sitting on the bow during a drag, or coiling a line as we rumbled up the creek, brought a sense of validation. The water itself was invested with a sweet and simple joy.

I was so happy in those days that even the fish houses smelled sweet. It is difficult, even for a raw deckhand on a bay boat, to resist the arrogance of the water. My arms and chest were growing with the work, and the boat's rhythms seemed synchronized with everything inside me.

Roy was stringing the last knots between my hands when we began to hear a low-pitched hum out in the darkness. Before I could ask what it was, flashing red and white lights appeared, and the beam of a spotlight shot down to the choppy surface. It was a low-flying helicopter, headed toward us from the south end of the channel.

"Looks like somebody drowned," Garland sniffed. "Prob-ably some tourist who didn't know what the fuck he was doing."

I was already accustomed to the shrimper's harsh judg-ments about the water and who belonged on it. Every shrimper knew that tourists, with their fancy boats and tan-ning lotion and spinning reels, belonged anywhere but on a bay where men had to make a living.

"I knew a guy caught two of 'em once," Garland said. "Two of 'em in the same fuckin' drag."

I wondered what he did with the bodies.

"Had to leave his net beside the boat till the Coast Guard came. Shot half his fuckin' day."

I asked Roy if he ever caught a dead man.

"Once," he muttered. "Crabs had already gotten to him pretty good. It's hell getting a dead man out of a net."

I looked at my hands under the webbing and compared them to Roy's. Mine were softer, of course, but they had aged a lot in my short time on the water. Everything was changing...six weeks earlier I would have blanched at his blithe reaction to death. But not anymore.

The helicopter flew over us, blinded us for a moment with its brilliant spot. Roy didn't need my hands any longer, so I watched the lights drift northward until I could see them no more.

Garland scratched his crotch while he puttered around the deck. Roy wrapped up his thread and stepped into the cabin to begin another day.

* * *

A heavy pre-dawn thunderstorm finally broke our work string at fifty-three days, but that day turned out to be more eventful than most.

After Roy came to the boat and told me to go home for some beauty sleep, I set out for Tina the Mermaid. I looked forward to Donna, Knuckles, coffee—and even the hair-of-the-dog crowd that lined up for beer at seven. It would be fun to lounge around the marina in the morning again, like a celebrity dropping in on his old neighborhood.

There had been some changes since the last time I opened the place with Donna. The new dock hand was Rodney Gene's son, a jut-jawed kid from Dallas whose mother thought he might straighten up if he spent a summer on the coast.

He seldom arrived at the bar before eight, and his habit of not showing up at all was putting a crimp in Donna and Leo's frolics.

That, of course, was fine with me. For unspoken but obvious reasons, Donna and I never made love on days she had climbed the stairs with Leo. But on the sporadic days when there was no dock hand to spell her at lunch, Donna bounced into my room when her shift ended, and we'd both bless Jaquita for keeping Sharlene an extra hour.

I didn't have Donna to myself, but at least I had her—and that was far better than the alternative. There was solace in the fact that she wanted me for simply being me, not because of what I gave her and not because I was good with the baby. Each time Donna appeared at my door, or gave me a private wink, or waved at me from the fuel dock, it was easy to wipe every bit of trouble from my mind.

Another big change on the docks involved Knuckles, who had lost his boat when the Pier Four discovered he was selling part of his catch in San Leon. Fletcher agreed to let Knuckles and Joe the Snake sleep on his boat while Knuckles opened oysters and looked for another boat to run.

After parking beneath Tina's slickened breasts, I strolled into the bar's familiar morning mildew and found Knuckles, soaked to the skin, perched on his favorite stool. I looked twice—something about him was different.

"Hello all," I said. "How about a steaming cup of vitamins for a rained-out pirate?"

Donna grinned and shoved her bar rag into my chest. "Clean them tables, boy, or are you too good to work here anymore?"

I started with the bar. Donna shuffled over to Knuckles and straightened a tuck in his collar.

"How you like this fella's new wardrobe?"

That was it. For the first time all summer, Knuckles had changed clothes. Black slacks and a short-sleeve white shirt—with the shirt tucked in.

"Holy quick-change, Batman. What's the occasion?"

"Job interview," Knuckles said proudly. "Fella from Houston's buying the Norton boat, and he needs a man to run it." He pulled a wet cigarette from his pack and decided against trying to light it. "Guess I'm kinda nervous."

"He's gonna knock him dead," Donna said. "I been telling him he's got nothing to worry about. Just turn on that old Knuckles charm and it's a cinch."

The rain made Tina's busier than usual that morning, with several idle shrimpers mixed in among the booze hounds. Knuckles' new wardrobe kicked the mumbling level up a few decibels. Everyone noticed the stir except him.

By eight o'clock I was wondering aloud where the dockhand was.

"He showed up two straight days," Donna said. "Probably figures he's due for a day off."

Donna had a sudden thought, and she leaned forward to whisper it.

"I know what Leo's gonna count on if he sees you here at lunchtime."

"I'll do whatever you want."

The lines on her face seemed to unravel. "Then vanish before he gets here, hot shot. My guess is Jaquita's gonna have a long afternoon."

As noon approached I moved my car behind the Paradise and waited at the bar there for Leo to hear the sad news and leave. The sky was clear and blue when he drove away.

Back at Tina's, Donna met me at the door with a beer and asked if I'd tend bar while she helped Bunny untangle the latest diesel invoice. I set my bottle next to Knuckles', and I noticed he was growing edgy.

"Better give me one more and a cup of coffee beside it," he said. "Boss man's gonna be here any minute, and I wanna be drinking something righteous when he shows."

The front door opened precisely at noon. A brightly dressed family of four crept in as if they were entering Dracula's castle. The patriarch, a late-thirties up-and-comer with white shorts and formless legs, was trying his best to look relaxed.

"Knucks, there's your man," I said. "Straight from the sportswear department."

Knuckles grabbed his coffee and asked me to stow his beer. Mrs. Down-from-Houston's eyes widened when Knuckles stood, and she took an unconscious step backward. She'd warned her husband about this.

The fellow shook Knuckles' hand and reached instinctively to shield the daughter nearest him. Both men bobbed and shrugged until Knuckles motioned toward the patio. A grim Mrs. Houston folded her arms and led the way.

They were still arranging chairs outside when the front door opened again, and I felt my boots melt onto the floor. Standing there, with a beard thicker and grayer than I remembered, was my father.

This was serious. He had gotten up early, taken the day off, and driven all the way down from Fort Worth. The easy confidence I'd developed over the past weeks was gone in an instant. Yet when our eyes met he seemed almost as startled as I.

"Sam!" He threw his arms around me. "How you doing, son?"

"Great, Dad. Great."

"Jesus, look at that tan. And those arms! But I expected to see you tonight, not now."

"Got rained out. I'm just running the bar awhile for a friend."

He climbed onto a stool and asked for my coldest brew. His smile was stiff and self-conscious—it was hard to watch him force such good cheer.

"What brings you down, Dad?"

He licked foam from his mustache and looked around the bar. "It's not every day a man loses his son to a brave new world. Thought I'd have a look at what it's like." He turned toward the bay. "I remember how you used to love fishing, Sam. I guess nowadays you're getting all the fishing you can stand."

"No complaints."

"No complaints, huh?" He smiled wryly. "I wonder if that's the highest and best use of a man's talent—finding a place where he's got no complaints."

"Aw, Dad, you're supposed to soften up the opponent, pepper him, make his arms heavy. You should save your best shot until he's reeling."

"I'm not here to pepper you, Sam."

Out on the patio, the Houstonian was perched eagerly on his chair, thrilled with the danger of talking to a weather-beaten old scoundrel. His wife and daughters were on the dock, tossing crackers up to the gulls.

"Your mother and I always had this fantasy, Sam. You were going to take over the shop, and we were going to move to a cabin somewhere and live the good life. Looks as if the roles got switched."

I shrugged uncomfortably.

"Alright, Sam, alright. Maybe you've got something here. Maybe a man ought to do what he wants, whenever he wants to do it."

"I know you too well," I said. "There's a `but' in there somewhere."

He worked at a smile. "It's just that you seem so casual about it all. Take it from somebody who knows: Weeks turn quickly into months, and months turn quickly into years—"

"—And before you know it," I said, "you've got corns and bursitis and nothing to look forward to but a lifetime of regret." I reached across and patted his arm.

"I know, Dad. I understand how worried you are. But I'm still young. Maybe I don't know what I'm doing, but at least I'm happy. I've only been out of school a couple of months, so I'm not exactly cutting it close."

There was motion on the patio. Knuckles opened the door and walked tentatively toward us. Outside, Mr. Houston wandered over to his wife and assured her everything was under control. *Honey, you can tell by the looks of him he's the best shrimper out here. I can deal with him. We're on the same wavelength...*

Knuckles slapped a twenty on the bar and lifted two crooked fingers.

"Michelob," he said sheepishly. "Boss man says nothing but the best."

"Well, Knucks, when Rome comes to visit, you've got to drink as the Romans drink."

"Gimme a sip of that other, Sam. It'll cut the taste."

I pulled out his half-empty Lone Star. Knuckles checked the patio and drained it in one pull. Then he nodded at my father.

"I'm Sam Traynor from Fort Worth," Dad said. "You a friend of my son's?"

Knuckles licked his tooth. "Oh, you bet—about the best friend I got going. I been knowing Sam quite a while now."

Dad answered with a pained smile.

"Say, Knucks," I said. "Think you got the job?"

"So far, so good," he said. "Got me a free beer out of it anyway, so it ain't no bust."

"He seems interested."

"And he can stay interested all day long, so long as he's buyin'—even if he's buyin' this."

Knuckles carried the bottles outside and smoothed the change on the table, as if he expected it to be counted. Mrs. Houston and the kids started walking to Tony Red's.

"I had this theory," Dad said. "I thought you'd get tired of this place unless you met some girl."

I had to laugh at that one.

"Yes, son, I guess that would be tough. This place probably isn't crawling with Phi Beta Kappas."

"One of its virtues, if you ask me."

Dad reached quickly for his beer. The conversation was getting away from him.

"Don't let your old man make you mad, son. I know you're doing what you gotta do."

What a difference a summer makes. The last time I'd heard him say that, I was fighting to stand up straight. Now it sounded pretty good.

Dad was on his second bottle when Donna walked in, radiating her soapwashed charisma. She drifted around the bar, gave me a playful hug and stole a sip of my beer.

"It's a beautiful world," she announced. "Thanks for holding the fort, Sam Boy."

My father and I exchanged silent glances.

"Dad, I want you to meet the most remarkable woman. Shake hands with Donna Bedicek."

Donna smiled broadly and offered her hand. Dad pressed it politely between his.

"Donna, I give you the best father on earth. He drove all the way down here to convince me I should go home."

She looked quickly at my father and then at me.

"And, Donna, what I've been telling him is, I've realized I'm already there."

Fifteen

Time skimmed along even faster after I decided to stay on the bay beyond summer. Life was a succession of quiet dawns and warm sunsets linked by work and effortless sleep. I was on the waterfront to make a life, not just a season. By mid-July, Roy had begun mentioning the day he might retire and—could it be true?—hire me to run the Silver Dollar in his stead.

Nevertheless, there were gaps in the firmament. Watching Donna drive home with another man was never easy, and neither was the tangled sense of dignity that moved her to take money from Leo instead of me. But Donna reminded me again and again to enjoy the act of enjoying and to stop fretting over imperfections in a happiness most people never know.

The colossal weight of plans and expectations had driven me to the bay in the first place, and with Donna's help I was finally climbing out from under them.

Despite all that—indeed, because of it—after the fateful night at Grady's I became almost a member of Donna's family. On the frequent nights when the four of us hopped beer joints together, Sharlene and I were inseparable.

She was not the first child to find me amusing after my second beer, but with her it went deeper than that, perhaps because we represented to one another the sibling we never had. I have never known such a happy child. She reminded me of the untapped joy that resides in a rubber band or a toilet paper tube. I introduced her to the quiet pleasure of fishing off a dock, and I dreamed of the day she'd be tall enough to play pool.

Fletcher, though he remained a virtual mute, also responded well to my presence on those nights. I treated him with a deference he had long since lost among the other shrimpers, and he actually began to wear his teeth from time to time. Donna told me that in the first two weeks we socialized together, Fletcher had more fun than he'd known in the previous year.

*   *   *

By late July the docks were abuzz with preparations for the annual street dance welcoming open season, the August liberation that bay shrimpers lived for. Open season meant the end of daily catch limits, and it allowed boats to replace their twenty-five-foot nets with hungrier forty-footers.

Maxwell and Adelia also welcomed the season with a boat parade and ceremonial blessing of the fleet. The blessing was a family affair with decorated boats, lawn chairs on decks and cheering multitudes on shore. And it was a soothing respite from the preceding night's dance, which traditionally was a tribute to public drunkenness and pugilism. Shrimpers and outsiders journeyed from all over the coast for that, and the creek was jammed with gulf boats whose layovers had been planned around the party.

Roy had no patience for the crowd and the parade on Sunday. That meant I would have the day off and could revel in the street dance Saturday night without a curfew. Maxwell and Adelia hosted the dance on alternating years, and this summer the arena was the narrow road along Adelia's side of the creek.

We spent the early hours of the dance on Tina's dock—Donna, Fletcher, Sharlene, and I. Sharlene was especially radiant, wearing a new lace halter and cotton shorts. The tiny pearls in her ears almost glistened, even in the dusk, against her summer tan.

Donna had celebrated my rare day off by springing for a fifth of Canadian. There was an understanding among us that we would last much longer at the dance if we waited until dark to cross the bridge. So we lazed together as the light slowly left us, four mismatched souls listening to the bursts of fireworks and whiskey bottles across the creek.

Sharlene was in my lap, painting my fingernails with a crayon, when I asked if she wanted something to drink.

"Two," she said, without looking up.

"Two of what?"

"Two."

Fletcher lumbered inside for a Coke, and when he put it on the table I had a sudden inspiration.

"Sharlene," I announced, "today is the day you're going to say your second word."

She set aside her crayon and reached out for the bottle. I drew it back.

"I wonder if you'd mind saying my name, Sharlene."

"Two."

"No, my real name: Sam."

She gave me a puzzled look, then reached vainly for the soda.

"Sam," I repeated. "S-A-M. You can do it."

"Two," she said irritably. "Two!"

"See this cool, beautiful, frosty bottle of Coke? Wouldn't you like to have a drink? All you have to do is say my name."

"You're wasting your breath," Donna said. "She's gonna talk when she's good and ready. And besides, when she does, her first new word's gonna be Donna."

"Sam, you mean.

"No, Donna."

"Sam."

"Donna."

"Sam."

"Donna."

Sharlene lunged across my lap and blurted "Dam!" before she snatched the bottle and took a greedy drink. Donna, Fletcher and I exchanged dumbfounded looks.

"Did you hear that?" I finally said. "Sharlene, sweetheart...what did you just say?"

She set the bottle aside and ceremoniously ignored the question.

"Did you say Sam?"

"No," Donna said. "There was a `D' in it. I'm sure I heard a `D'.

"Say it again, Sharlene. Sam. Sam."

She found her crayon and returned to my nails.

"You meant Donna, didn't you? Go ahead, say Donna."

"Nope, she meant Sam. Three letters, one syllable. No doubt about it."

Donna turned to Fletcher. "You heard it," she said. "Tell Sam here she was calling my name."

Fletcher shrugged, looking vaguely hurt.

"Come on, you can't weasel out of this one. Tell us what she said."

He shrugged again, then rasped, "Cuss word."

"What?"

"She was cussing you both out."

We all turned to Sharlene, and the impish smile on her face proved Fletcher had it right.

"Why you..." Donna said. "You've been holding out on us, haven't you?"

Sharlene blushed and ran to Fletcher's lap.

"You can talk, but you've just been faking it all this time."

"But why?" I asked.

"Just to make us work harder, isn't that it, rascal?"

She giggled as she hid her face in Fletcher's shirt.

"Well, how do you like that?" Donna said. "She's had our number all along, just toying with us."

"Well," I said, "we'd better start watching what we say around her. She's liable to blab it all over the docks."

"The wonders never cease, Sam. But congratulations. You're the one who finally cracked the code."

*   *   *

Parking was so scarce by the time we crossed the creek, we

had to walk several blocks to the party. Sharlene reached up to me on tiptoe, and I lifted her for a shoulder ride. The four of us strolled on, and when the balloons and snapping flags came into view, Sharlene unclasped my hair just long enough to raise her fists and shout a delirious "Two!"

"Don't you mean `damn'?" I asked. "—or Sam, or maybe `What a smashing spectacle.'"

"Two," she replied breathlessly. "Two, two, two!"

"Oh well, we'll take our progress where we can get it," Donna said. And then, suddenly inspired by the sights, she rushed ahead and motioned for us to stop.

"Here goes nothing." She reached into her purse for the bottle, drained an inch from it, then pressed a dainty spot of liquor behind each ear. "Yes!" she growled, "The fragrance no man can resist." Then she capped the fifth, threw it twenty feet in the air and caught the neck easily in one hand.

"Two!" Sharlene squealed, clapping her tiny hands. Donna holstered the bottle in her purse and walked nonchalantly ahead.

Of all the marvels and pleasures of the waterfront, this incomparable woman represented the pinnacle. I fancied thinking that Donna had blossomed in the weeks I'd known her, becoming ever more relaxed, open, self-assured. Certainly it was more than the daily salve of a summer on the bay, or even an affair with a younger man, that made her shoulders move so freely.

I wanted to believe that by confiding in her—and by nudging her to confide in me—I had brought her farther out of herself. I know we both very much enjoyed what we saw. I had fallen in love with Donna for many reasons, but none more than this: She seemed to prove everything I wanted to believe about this place, and about my place in it. Almost singlehandedly, she had justified my decision to come here—and to stay.

* * *

Fletcher eventually took a gulp from the bottle and paid for it with a choking fit that turned heads for fifty yards around. Donna pointed slyly to her mouth, relieved that he'd left his teeth at home. Sharlene squealed a couple of joyful twos while Donna slapped Fletcher on the back. He looked up, crimson-faced, and passed the bottle to me.

"Take a lesson from hotshot," Donna said. "Don't try to get drunk in one swig."

Men and women were milling on the street and wandering from booth to booth, here buying a beer and a setup, there spilling them on one another. Children and dogs scampered under the stringed light bulbs, kicking up dust as they looked for something new to explore. The stench of the waterfront was shrouded now with the happy smells of garlic, Tabasco, buttered corn—and everywhere the sticky bouquet of beer.

We passed circles of men, standing in fours and fives with their thumbs hooked in their back pockets. The posture everywhere was rural—bodies cocked at the waist, a boot scuffing at a pebble on the ground.

"So I told the sumbitch, you do that again and I'll..."

"No fuckin' way I'm puttin' up with that shit..."

"I told him I'd a tore his fuckin' arm off..."

"That's pure-dee bullshit, man. Pure-dee fuckin' shit..."

Fletcher stopped at a beer stand and I drifted in behind him. He handed me a can and pointed to a small crowd gathering behind a fish house.

The stir was soon attracting notice all along the road. Antsy men craned for a look, then patted their women's shoulders and told them to wait right there while they checked it out.

"Fist fight," Donna said. "Best thing is to stay away so you don't get ticked with a stray knuckle."

"No can do," I told her. "I haven't seen a live fight since junior high."

I lowered Sharlene to the oyster shell. Fletcher fell in step behind me and sucked foam from the top of his beer. We squeezed in among some shoulders, and I felt an evil thrill—

the combatants were female. The aggressor was a spike-haired woman in her fifties wearing rhinestone sunglasses and knee-length shorts.

"I'll teach you to go tearing up my husband's boat," she snarled.

"But I wasn't!" the other woman whimpered. "I was just looking!"

"Yeah, just looking with a goddamn buck knife in your hand. You were getting ready to cut a piece of net to decorate your fucking garage."

The other woman, clearly guilty and just as clearly drunk, searched the crowd with crazed eyes. She was a short stump of a woman and clearly no match for her captor.

"Will somebody help me?" she shrieked. "This crazy woman's gonna kill me."

"You shouldn't orta ruin a man's net," someone in the crowd said. "That's his living, lady. It ain't right."

That stirred an approving murmur. The accused woman began to breath audibly.

"So," she sputtered to no one in particular, "I'm gonna get my ass stomped, right here, just like that?"

A chill went through the assembly. Everyone was focused on the spike-haired woman. She began to lose her taste for battle.

"No, you ain't gonna get stomped," she said. "But you *are* gonna go for a swim."

The crowd erupted into whoops and whistles.

"No!" the woman pleaded, tugging at her cotton T-shirt. "I ain't got nothing on underneath."

"If you ain't in the creek by the count of three, I'm gonna launch your miserable ass myself. One—"

"Please!"

"Two—"

She landed in a noisy splash and came to the surface with black hair slapped flat over her eyes.

"You bitch," she shrieked. "You satisfied now?"

"Yeah, darlin'. Don't go out too far now, or the current'll

get you. There's a shallow spot over here when you're ready to get out."

She turned to the crowd.

"OK people, let's give the lady some privacy. She's took her medicine."

Back at the road, Donna had Sharlene on one hip and the bottle open for us. Fletcher took a short pull and seemed refreshed.

"Don't know about y'all," Donna said. "Me and Sharlene are so hungry, we're about to cave in."

Fletcher took another swallow of whiskey and shook his head. Donna laughed at him and fussed with a tangle in Sharlene's hair.

"He don't want to mess up his drunk," she said. "How about you, Sam?"

We stopped at a shrimp booth a few yards from the bandstand and started peeling supper at a picnic table. Sharlene, as always, was fascinated by the severed heads.

"No," Donna said. "Them's for the crabs to eat. Here, try the meat instead."

Sharlene tightened her lips.

"Suit yourself." Donna tossed a shrimp high in the air and caught it in her mouth. Sharlene applauded merrily and spent the rest of the meal throwing shrimp heads at passersby.

It soon became clear that Fletcher was bewitched by the booze. His eyes were more alive than usual, and his head even began to bob with the music. Suddenly he cleared his throat and said, "You know, I practically killed myself on the boat this morning."

Donna and I looked at one another, dumb struck. It was the first time all summer I'd heard him utter a complete, unprompted sentence.

"That damn Joe. He moved from his regular hiding place, and I nearly broke my back tripping over him."

"Knuckles' snake?" Donna said. "Why's he still on your boat?"

"That Houston guy won't let Knuckles keep it, ever since

he pulled that stunt on him about getting something out from the bunk. The owner likes to go on the boat sometimes, and he's afraid Joe's gonna eat his leg off."

Donna's eyes brightened.

"So Knuckles can sleep on the boat in the same clothes for three months, but Joe's gotta go?"

"That's how come I got him," Fletcher said sadly.

*   *   *

"Adension lady and gernelmen!"

Everyone looked up. A voice, a bullhorn, was above us.

"Is evernbuddy have a goo time?"

Someone pointed to a giant gulf shrimper. "Look! Up on the stabilizer!"

There, wobbling in the milky moonlight, was a human silhouette. A man was clinging to the metal rigging about forty feet above the dock.

"I wan take this 'tunity to welcome y'all to the werl-famus street daynce. This is—"

The bullhorn glinted briefly before it crashed to the dock. The man was holding himself on the rigging with one arm and swinging three beer cans by their plastic collar with the other.

"It's Amos," Donna explained. "He spends almost his whole life on the gulf, which is probably a good thing. He never drinks out there."

A couple of men hurried over to coax Amos down. They shouted and waved their arms for a couple of fruitless minutes and then scattered like bugs when Amos began relieving himself in their direction.

"Nothing beats a good party, right gal?"

It was the putative Dr. Von Fistfurt, standing behind Donna with his hands on her shoulders. Judging by his accent and demeanor, he was appearing tonight in the person of wildcatter Oran Bowman.

"Nothing I love better than good company in the great

out-of-doors. How about yourself, gal?"

Donna reached up and patted his hands.

"You got it, Oran."

He was well past his eight beers now, puffed-up and pop-eyed and swaying like a happy cow. His stethoscope was askew and hanging by one earpiece. Donna stood up to straighten it.

"Can't have you losing this," she said. "Dr. Von would throw a hissy."

Oran nodded casually and surveyed the street as though he owned it. Bowman had become my favorite of all his incarnations because of his habit of buying beer for every man, woman and child he addressed.

"What y'all drankin'?" he said. "Ready for another round?"

I was dispatched with a five dollar bill to fetch beer. Standing in line, I looked back to see Oran kiss Sharlene on top of her head and then wander away. Then there was a sudden flash of paisley and Bunny Hogner's frowning face in mine.

"Where is she?" Her breath dried the moisture from my eyes. "I got something for Donna that's gonna stir her fuckin' hash."

"Sorry," I said, "haven't seen her."

"Don't lie to me, Sam. I know you two are asshole buddies. If you're here, she can't be far away."

Bunny lumbered around me and headed toward the creek. I watched her stop at a booth for a set-up and then spike it with a flask.

I'd spent much of the summer avoiding her, because I knew she resented my friendship with Donna. Sometimes when she saw me in a bar, Bunny mouthed the word "stolen" and broke into her yellow smile.

She slipped the flask back into her purse and looked at me with such malignant satisfaction that I felt myself straighten. That was the face she tortured me with in bars, and now she was looking for Donna. When she found the table and headed for it, Sharlene was asleep in Donna's lap.

Bunny sat next to them heavily and pulled something from her purse. Where was Fletcher? Donna read what Bunny gave her and looked up in a panic. I ran over, and when she saw me, Donna seemed to lose strength.

"What's going on?" I demanded.

Bunny pulled a post card from Donna's hand. "This, buddy boy, is what's going on."

The card was addressed in pencil to Donna, care of the marina, in crude block letters.

I know you done good by my baby. I thank you for it too. But do you know what it does to a mother to be away from her flesh and blood. When I came to get Sharlene you understood. It was Fletch that stoped it. Will you please help me get my baby back. If you dont I got to call the cops. Judith.

Donna shuddered when I handed back the card. Her gray eyes looked deep inside me.

And I knew I would never see her again.

Sixteen

On Sunday my eyes opened to a wide blue morning window. The sky over Tina's was graced with floating gulls and drifting puff clouds. For the first time since I'd come to the bay, the sun had risen without me. And for the first time in weeks I had a brief glimpse of this place as a stranger might see it.

The creek seemed weary now, even sullen in the littered aftermath of the dance. The booths on the Adelia shore were deserted, wearing limp crepe and drooping balloons. The blessing of the fleet was still hours away, and I imagined everyone else sprawled in bed as I was, asking why it is that wonderful things must always end so quickly.

The best thing ever to visit my life was gone. I knew that from this day forward, I would be truly on my own. Donna had taken to a highway somewhere, running with Sharlene and Fletcher to a safer place. She didn't know where they would go and wouldn't have told me if she did. Even now there was still too much of the outsider about me, and too much of the wolf in her, to abide that risk.

Maybe they were rolling north just then on Houston's giant freeways, staring up at the skyscrapers from their overloaded Falcon, scared and bewildered and thinking that if only...

I sat up and opened the window. Fletcher's boat was tied at the fuel dock, swaying ungracefully on a fretful tide. No one was on it now but Joe the snake, if that. The boat would float there like a ghost ship for hours, maybe even a day or two, until someone told the owner it was abandoned. That damned sure wouldn't be me. I'd spent a summer keeping quiet about more important things than that. I wasn't even going to tell Bunny or Rodney Gene that the marina was still locked on what would be the busiest day of the year. Donna was on the highway now, and Donna needed time.

*   *   *

After I had read the post card the night before, Donna turned sharply from Bunny and folded it in half. Sharlene stirred in her lap, her earrings glinting from beneath her hair. Bunny reached for her flask and sneered at me.

"And you thought I was lyin', didn't ya Sam?"

I watched Donna lick her thumb to sponge a crumb from Sharlene's mouth. No, I hadn't thought Bunny was lying. I never faced it completely until that moment, but in the darkest corner of my soul I had always thought Donna was the liar.

"Didn't ya, Sam? Didn't ya?"

I turned away, but Bunny lunged for my arm.

"I'm talking to you," she said. "I say you knew it all along."

"Shut up, you fat fuck, or I'll shove that flask down your throat."

"You did know! You did! You knew it was true, and you didn't do nothing about it!"

I slapped at the flask, and it landed in a brittle crash between us.

"You little slime," she snarled. "I had you figured for the kind who'd do something about it. You, the fuckin' soul-searcher from the great big college. Well, ha! You're no different from the rest of 'em. You're just another piece of scum from the docks!"

Bunny shoved me aside and stalked away. I sat beside Donna without looking at her.

"I need to find Fletcher," she finally said. She shaped Sharlene into a transferable bundle and asked me to hold her while she looked.

Donna left her purse behind, and I reached inside, hoping the Canadian would settle the moil within me. I looked down at the baby whose life I had done so little and so much to shape, and her eyelids fluttered with an innocent's dreams.

She was so beautiful, with her soft face laid open before me. I brushed back her hair, wishing I could squeeze her to me and whisper into her lovely ears the truth. I wanted to tell her everything I knew, everything, so that *she* could decide.

I must have held her too close, or perhaps I was shaking, because Sharlene began to stir. Her eyelids parted for an instant, just long enough to recognize me, and she fell back asleep with a gentle smile.

"It's Sam," I whispered, "your buddy. Tell me, sweetheart, what am I supposed to do?"

"Well, I found him—for whatever it's worth."

Fletcher was swaying beside Donna, his eyelids drooping under a euphoric weight. He was beyond caring about the postcard, probably even beyond understanding it.

"We need to get off the street," Donna said. "There's no telling when she's gonna show."

So, I thought, *Donna's made the move for us.*

"Let's hit one of those bars back by the bridge," she said. "It's time to get some coffee into Gregory Peck, here."

Donna nestled Sharlene against her shoulder and handed her purse to Fletcher. Then she took the bottle out and slipped it to me.

"Here," she whispered. "We'll be a lot better off if you keep an eye on this."

Fletcher looked at the booze forlornly, and I waited until he fell into step behind Donna before I tilted it again. Our wavering caravan came finally to a screened-in beer joint called Lacy's. Donna laid the baby beside her in a booth while Fletcher and I squeezed in across the table.

The waitress sighed peevishly when Donna ordered coffee

for two. Sobriety held no great promise for me at that moment, so I asked for a setup.

Donna took a few seconds to size up Fletcher, who was already melting into the vinyl. Then she regathered her hair into a pony tail, looking straight at me.

"You know we've got to leave," she said.

Hearing the words took the air from me, and all I could manage was a weak shudder. Donna stirred Fletcher's coffee and seemed surprised I hadn't challenged the plan.

"Where?" I said numbly.

"Don't know. All I know is, it can't be around no shrimping towns, or she'll track us down."

I poured too much Canadian into my glass, and Donna dropped a spoonful of it in hers. I knew what I wanted to say, but Fletcher wasn't fully asleep yet. This was all happening too fast, Donna going, Sharlene's mother, losing Donna, stolen girl...

After a clumsy silence Donna whispered, "I'm sorry for what Bunny did to you."

"Don't talk about that," I snapped. Then I heard myself think aloud, "She looks down her nose at me for doing nothing, but what has she done?"

The implication hurt Donna perceptibly. "But you done *right*, Sam. If you weren't sure before what kind of woman Sharlene's momma was, you oughta be now."

I almost swooned in relief. *Of course.* The post card proved everything I wanted to believe but hadn't. Donna's version was true, the girl's mother was a louse, and yes, Sharlene was where she belonged. I had done the right thing for the wrong reasons, but at least I had done what was right.

Donna reached again for the bottle, and I watched Fletcher's head come slowly to rest against the wall. I must have stared too long.

"You never understood why I stayed with him," she said.

"I imagine everybody on the creek wonders the same thing."

I looked at my glass and tried to summon some courage.

"Sometimes I even wonder, Sam. I mean, look at him. He's

the same way my Daddy was, a strong man who lost whatever made him strong. I don't know. Maybe I think I can do a
better job this time." She smiled sadly. "Listen to that shit. I'm
starting to sound like Sam the Philosopher."

Sharlene turned in her sleep and stretched her arms across
Donna's lap. Donna studied Fletcher for a moment before she
spoke again.

"He ain't gonna react too good when he hears what's going on. Life hasn't exactly been kind to Fletcher Quinn the last
couple years."

I took a deep breath and leaped.

"Dump him, Donna. Lose the son of a bitch. You give him
too much credit. Maybe he's a nice guy, but hell, every time I
see that scar on your face—"

Donna looked at me sharply. "It's been a two-way street,
you know. Listen, more than anybody else, you ought to
know I ain't been no saint. Maybe I deserve what I get."

"That's great. Guilt and pity are fine pillars for a relation-
ship. Why don't you stop letting him punish you? You don't
have to take this."

Donna smiled as though I had just figured it out.

"You're exactly right, Sam. And that's why I do."

I slumped back in my seat. Donna had ruled out staying
with me before I could even ask. And why? For the sake of the
lazy quitter snoring beside me.

"Goddamn it, Donna. This is insane. You're leaving the
water, giving up everything—your whole life—for a bum
who'll only drag you down."

Donna's eyes began to fill, but I wouldn't stop.

"You told me yourself you were willing to give Sharlene
back to her mother once. It was only Fletcher who stood in the
way.

"So leave him, Donna. Leave him and stay with me. We
can keep Sharlene, give her up—I don't care. All I can think
about is us. You're doing all this because that bastard wants it,
not you."

Fletcher folded his arms with an audible effort, then drifted away again without opening his eyes. Donna tried vainly to steady her coffee cup and then finally pushed it away.

"You're wrong. It ain't got nothing to do with Fletcher." She looked down to the delicate creature beside her. "I've learned a lot of things from you, Sam, and one of them is that people can change. If this had happened before I met you…yes, I probably would have let her go. But not anymore, Sam. Now I'd die first."

"Fine, then. We keep her. We raise her—sure. But it's going to be you and me."

Donna reached for my hands. "Sam, face it. It wouldn't work. It would be hard enough, even if you wanted Sharlene more than anything in the world. But we both know you don't."

"Now you're wrong."

"Come on, Sam. You proved it with everything you just said."

I couldn't believe it. Whatever I'd persuaded her of that summer, whatever I'd done—it had moved Donna to keep a baby from a mother who wanted her back. And I was losing her because of it.

A loud stir erupted in the parking lot and spread inside near the door. People left their seats, then quickly took them again as Knuckles bounded in with Joe the snake looped about his shoulders. He spotted our table and strutted toward us, stunningly unaware of the commotion he had caused.

"Hey evrabody!" He was swaying under the unbalanced weight of the snake. "Hey evrabody, one and all!"

Knuckles pulled up an empty chair and tossed the snake's tail over his shoulder, the way flying aces flick their scarves.

"Hey, Knucks," Donna said gamely, pulling her hands away.

Knuckles lifted the snake's head and with a giant forefinger stroked it between the eyes. Then he pointed to a bulge a few inches behind its neck.

"Joe had him a big meal tonight, and he wanted to walk it off."

"You don't normally take him out," Donna sighed.

"Yeah, but he's been kinda depress lately. Figured he could use him some fresh air."

The bartender appeared from the darkness, keeping a respectful distance from Joe.

"Sorry, Knucks," he said. "The snake's gotta go. My customers are to too scared to drink. And besides, I think it's against my license or something."

Knuckles drew Joe's head away as if to shield him from the news.

"All right, we'll be goin'. It's too much smoke in here for Joe anyhow."

There were a couple of fingers of booze left, and I asked Knuckles if he'd dispose of it for us. He tucked the bottle into the crook of his arm as if it were a gurgling newborn.

"You's good people, Sam. Real good people."

He strolled outside like a king descending his throne. From the window I saw him drain the bottle in one pull and invite Joe to explore it with his tongue. The snake wasn't interested, so Knuckles dropped it in a small burst behind himself.

When finally I was able to look at Donna again, she was spinning her cup in small turns on the table.

"Strange," she blurted. "I can't stop thinking about my momma—and how every time I look at you I see her."

In my reeling brain I saw a cotton dress slapped wet against a pubic bone, a spoiled and willful victim...

"Back on the farm she didn't know what she wanted, really. All she knew was that she wanted out. But there was one thing she was sure of. Momma knew she wasn't going to drown in the same shit that gets everybody else.

"I don't know if you want to hear this, Sam, but I'll never get another chance to tell you. I mean what I said about me changing this summer on account of you. Remember how I always said plans and dreams were nothing but trouble? I really believed that. I saw where plans and hopes got my mother—and I remembered where they got me when Fletcher and me had it good.

"But then you came along, all fresh and excited, eager to get on a boat and learn about the water. You made Momma come alive again."

I shook my head impatiently. "You've got it all wrong, Donna. I came here scared out of my mind because I *didn't* have any plans. Don't you see? I was losing my wits by the minute *because* of plans. And you were right. It took you to teach me how to take life as it comes.

"And that's what I'm going to do—with you. You and me—and Sharlene—together, no expectations, just living and letting the world come to us. That's all that matters."

"Sam, it's not enough to just survive for another day. That's when you get kicked around—the way my Daddy got kicked, and the way I've been kicked all my life. Well, I'm through living like a goddamn animal. I've got something to live for now."

She reached down and smoothed Sharlene's halter.

"Hey, look at me, Sam! I've got plans!"

"Donna, listen—"

"Sorry, I won't. I've made up my mind. I'm going to leave, and that's all there is to it. I'm taking Fletcher with me, and there's no way around that, neither. Sharlene would die without him—and it's better for you, too. I don't want you mixed up in this mess. You're still a young man, Sam. You need your freedom—and you need this place—a hell of a lot more than you need us."

"No!"

Fletcher awoke in a start and tipped over his coffee. The commotion roused Sharlene, who sat up and splashed her hands in the puddle. After the waitress had cleaned the mess, Donna reached into her purse and handed Fletcher the post-card.

"Where'd you get this?" he said groggily. "What's going on?"

Donna pulled out a brush and began running it through Sharlene's hair.

"Bunny delivered it this evening," she said. "Looks like

you-know-who has changed her mind again."

"Shit." Fletcher still wasn't fully alert. "What we gonna do?"

"We're gonna leave, is what we're gonna do. Tonight, first thing, just as soon as you get your head screwed on straight."

It took a moment for the words to sink in, but when they did, Fletcher looked at me desperately.

"Wait a minute. What...what the hell you talking about?"

Sharlene slipped under the table and out into the bar.

"I'm talkin' about she means business this time, and she probably won't fall for no heroics when she finds us. We got to get gone, and we got to do it now."

Fletcher rubbed his face. The absolute, disastrous finality of it all was too much to comprehend.

"But...my boat...open season," he said. "I'll miss half the damn season looking for a boat somewhere else."

"Ain't gonna be no more boats," Donna said firmly. "We'll be sitting ducks if we go anywhere there's shrimpers. She'll find us sure as hell."

Fletcher flung his head from side to side.

"Wait a goddamn minute," he said. "What the hell am I supposed to do?"

"You're gonna get a regular job, is what you're gonna do." Donna leaned forward as though she had rehearsed the speech for years. "You're gonna work every day, the way a man's supposed to. No more tearing up a boat so you can cool your heels. You're gonna start pulling your weight and help us build a life."

The words pummeled him like stones. After all, it was he who had the most to lose. Three decades of work, a way of life, his identity, every last scrap of satisfaction—it was all being snatched away. Sharlene, unaccustomed to such animation in Fletcher, pointed at him and shouted, "Two! Two!" as if he were performing at her birthday party.

"Shut up!" he snapped.

"Two! Two!"

He grabbed at her outstretched arm, then quickly stopped

himself, but it was enough to frighten her. Sharlene sprawled face-down in the aisle.

"I don't like it," Fletcher barked. But his resolve was evaporating quickly. "Running, giving up everything, I don't know...just to hide from that fool woman."

Donna cleared her throat calmly.

"You got any better ideas?"

"No!" Fletcher squeezed his head in anguish. "I don't know what—"

Everyone at the table froze. Standing above us was Leo, unsteady with drink and scowling at Fletcher like a prison guard. He leaned toward Donna and said, "Any problems here, darlin'?"

Donna was so astonished that she couldn't answer. Leo turned his face to Fletcher.

"Maybe if you treated her halfway decent, she wouldn't have to find comfort with another man."

Donna's mouth fell open. Leo grinned smugly, and Fletcher immediately grasped the significance of what he'd heard.

"You goddamn fucks!" Fletcher reached across me and grabbed Donna and Leo by their collars. "I'm gonna kill you both!"

The bar filled with panicked murmurs and scraping chairs. Someone shouted for the police. My face was engulfed in the salty darkness of Fletcher's armpit, but I could hear the crunch of hurried feet on the shell outside.

"Just take it easy," Donna said evenly. "Ain't nobody gonna kill nobody. Just cool yourself off, Fletch, before they come lock you up."

I leaned away and saw Leo's eyes dart from Donna to Fletcher and back again. He was sober enough now to know he'd bitten off too big a hunk.

"No problem," he gasped. "I got no problems with no-body."

Fletcher flung him loose and tightened his grip on Donna's shirt. She steeled herself, but a spasm under her eye told me she'd seen Fletcher this way before. Leo turned to leave, and Fletcher ordered him to freeze. He stopped with one foot in front of the other.

"Donna!" Fletcher was livid, but in his voice there was the faint trace of a whimper. "Him?"

She looked away. Fletcher's sleeve began to quiver, and he suddenly shouted, "What's happening to me!" He let Donna go and looked at his hand in disbelief.

"Nothing's changed," Donna said. She reached for Fletcher's hand and stroked it slowly. "We've still got to go, you and me, or we lose her."

Fletcher tilted his head toward Leo.

"And this guy?"

"Gone."

Leo sighed in obvious relief. Donna reached over to his forearm and said, "Go on, Leo. You better leave now." He was through the door in three steps.

Donna looked out into the bar and realized our table was still drawing too much attention.

"Let's get out of here," she said. "We're liable to blow everything before we even get started."

She lifted Sharlene from the floor and began cuddling away her stiff resolve. By the time we reached the parking lot, the baby had her arms draped around Donna's neck and was drifting back to sleep.

Fletcher's boat was docked in a marina not far from my car, and there was an awareness among all of us that he was passing it for the last time. He had been scuffing listlessly at the roadway, but suddenly he stood erect.

"Hey," he said. "Let's go for a ride."

Donna and I looked at one other in disbelief. Her mere presence on Fletcher's own boat had once been enough to break his spirit. Now he was inviting a woman and a little girl aboard for the ultimate sacrilege—a pleasure cruise.

"I don't get it," Donna said. "Did I hear you right?"

Fletcher shoved his hands in his pockets. "I said let's go for a ride."

Donna pressed Sharlene's face into her shoulder and whispered, "We can't get where we're going on a boat. You know we're going inland."

"Inland, yeah, inland," Fletcher snapped. "You're the boss. But if I got to give up every damn thing, well...I ain't going nowhere without I get one last ride on the boat."

Donna seemed to forget the immediate problem. She bounced Sharlene to her other shoulder and vented a long-standing hurt.

"What happened to all that shit you used to spout? I thought it wasn't right for a lowly woman to be on a man's boat."

"Yeah," Fletcher said, "I used to have some big ideas, didn't I? Like maybe I was a man or something."

"Or something."

Fletcher cinched up his pants. He was using every last ounce of his strength and authority—all in an effort to make his humiliation complete.

"We're going for a ride," he said sternly. "You, me, and Sharlene are going for a ride on that boat."

He looked at me and dipped his head.

"You understand, Sam. It's a family deal, a ceremony like. We'll be all right."

Fletcher stepped over to a beer stand and put half a dozen cans in a bag. I whispered to Donna that she should come with me, right then. But she shook her head with a surprising serenity.

"You aren't worried?" I said.

"Naw. Couple hours on the water won't matter none. Hell, it'll probably calm him down."

There was only one chance left.

"Don't leave, Donna. We've got something. I see the whole world with new eyes since I met you. And you, you've said yourself what a difference I've made to you. Please, don't throw all that away."

Donna stole a glance at Fletcher and then looked up to me. "We have changed, Sam, both of us. But that's just it. We've changed too much."

Fletcher limped up and tossed me a beer from the sack. "Take it easy," he said abruptly. "It's been nice knowing you."

He lifted Sharlene and started off to the boat like a proud father walking to a picnic. Donna watched them fade into the shadows and then reached for me. We held each other as close as our arms would bring us, and then I felt her soft, pursed lips at my ear.

"I'm gonna miss you more than anyone I've known," she whispered. "Someday you'll know this is right. Now listen, Sam. When I let you go, don't say a word. I know everything you're thinking, but don't say it."

She slipped free and ran for the boat without looking back. I watched the white outline of her shoulders disappear and remembered the first time I saw that lovely apparition in the darkness outside the marina.

We were such different creatures then. It was because of her that I had a chance to taste the richness of life and to find myself as a man. And because of me, she was risking her survival for a plan, a purpose, an emotion, a little girl.

Fletcher's diesel roared to life, and I watched the rigging move slowly away from the dock. As the boat passed under a floodlight, I could see Donna crouched down with Sharlene on the stern, both of them waving goodbye toward the shadows where I stood.

Our time together had made something new of each of us, and the changes were now driving us apart. But because of her, I would be able to stand on my own in this place, braced by the strength and peace she'd helped me find.

Donna...the magnificent Donna. I watched her drift from my life knowing that she had shown me, and I had shown her, how to live.

Seventeen

It lands headfirst on the deck, bone against wood, with a dull wet-lumber thud. A glint of skin, slick and bruised. A blanket of shrimp and crab.

no

The net swings overhead, dripping brine onto the pile. Sea gulls gather, the engine revs higher. Roy shouts back how'd we do that time?

no

You remember to retie the bag. You fumble with the line as if you've never held it before. You reach for the winch and tell yourself

that was not, was not, what you saw

"I said was it a good drag?"

Roy is at the cabin door, debating whether to stay north or double back. You look at him blankly, not sure you want him to see.

guilty

Roy yawns, says it doesn't look bad. He moves inside and you are alone on deck, alone with the pile.

driftwood

yes

driftwood

You stick the rake in and pull shrimp away. Something is in there. Something

A hand, pink and blue, going bleary.

no

You pull more fish away. A patch of bloated skin, roadmap blotchy, red and blue and green. Tangled hair, white hair soaked brown, face down on the deck. A baby, the hairless slit of a girl, cloth stretched tight above the belly.

what was she wearing

Crabs pick at the face, a torn cheek, the snarl of exposed teeth.

She moves.

Slipping across the deck, slipping in the goo toward a scupper.

stop it

grab it

get it now it's all your fault

You clutch at her wrists and lift up. She stares at you, one eye bulging and one eye eaten away. You flinch, the skin on her hands slips off. She bounces on the gunwale and slices into the water without a sound.

You look at your hands, holding the skin from hers, delicate little gloves with pink fingernails.

There is nothing in the world but her face, staring up as it disappears under the waves.

the lidless eye

the open cheek

the tiny pearl earring still pinned into place

*   *   *

The official files show it was Jimmy Spencer, not I, who caught Sharlene's body in his shrimp net and then lost it moments later. We were miles away, on the north end of the ship channel, when it happened. Yet Jimmy's ghastly discovery has fueled my nightmares ever since.

Roy and I learned about it on the radio, then watched as the Coast Guard raced by to pick up the skin fragments. The authorities spent the rest of Monday afternoon on what they knew would be a fruitless search. Bodies caught by shrimpers are usually at rest on the bottom, which meant Sharlene's abdominal gases had not yet expanded enough to bring her to the surface.

On Wednesday, a kid on a catamaran found what was left of the body washed up on Redfish Island. Crabs and other scavengers had assaulted the softest tissues, stripping every identifying feature from the face—even the ears. But the coroner determined that the skin which came off in Jimmy's hands was a certain match.

Nevertheless, the police quickly despaired of making a positive identification. There were no relevant missing-person reports, no medical or dental records, no next of kin to be found. There was nothing but the disjointed account of a deck hand dazed by what he had found and so quickly lost again.

Had Fletcher taken his boat near Redfish? He didn't say where he was going when he left the dance Saturday night. Where did Donna go when they got back to shore? There was no way I could know.

The police didn't have what they wanted, but everyone on the waterfront knew who the dead girl was.

That little white-headed kid, you know the one. The kid that Donna was raising.

How can you be sure?

She was so eat up they couldn't tell. But Jimmy seen an earring on her, when she still had her ears on. You know damn well that's who it was.

* * *

I was recovering from a session in the sheriff's office when there was a sharp knock at my dockside door. Downstairs, I found Bunny squinting in the sunlight.

"Sam," she snapped, swinging the door open wide. "I want you to meet Judy Cason. She's Sharlene's momma."

Bunny didn't have to tell me who Judy Cason was. It was obvious from the wispy white hair and the pleasant turn of her earlobes. Bunny smiled at me with a sick satisfaction.

"Pleased to meet you," Judy said. "I understand you're close to Donna and my girl."

"Damn straight," Bunny said. "Him and Donna was asshole buddies all summer. He knew all about everything."

I expected that to tighten Judy's face, but she only nodded. "I don't imagine you've heard the best things about me."

Bunny crossed her arms and frowned in mock concern.

"She don't know nothing about nothing, Sam. Just pulled in here thirty seconds ago. I figured you ought to be the one to fill her in."

Bunny turned on a wobbly heel and stalked back to the office. Judy looked up at me apologetically. I invited her in for some air conditioning and followed her up the stairs.

It turned out that Sharlene's mother was a twenty-two-year-old girl with chewed cuticles and a pained, reflexive smile. She wore scuffed tennis shoes and jeans that had become too tight. Her faded peasant blouse was pasted to her back with perspiration. By the top of the stairs, she was out of breath.

"It's cool in here," I told her. She looked around my room uncertainly until I brought in a chair from the attic. Then she sat and lit a cigarette while I settled on a corner of the bed. We both fidgeted.

"Looks like I'm late," Judy finally said. She drew on her cigarette and exhaled at the ceiling. Her lips had Sharlene's fleshy pout.

"Bunny told me Donna split the minute she got my card."

"What else did Bunny say?"

"That you were the one who could help me find her."

I felt my chest sink.

"It was dumb to send that card, I know. Don't ask me how come I did it. I thought Donna would understand, not run off like a thief." Suddenly, she seemed to chafe at being on the defensive. "Oh, hell...maybe I wanted her to run off."

Judy seemed as startled by the admission as I and began stubbing out the cigarette on her sneaker.

"Hell, I don't mean that. It's just, well, I've really messed up my life and I don't know if I can ever make it right again.

But I'm gonna try."

I remembered Donna's account of the half-hearted martyr who had brought Sharlene into the world. "Why?" I blurted. "Doing your penance?"

She looked down at her cigarette, the color draining from her face. "What do you mean?"

I began pacing between the door and the bed. I had no business scolding anyone.

"Please help me," she said desperately. "Bunny tells me you was close with Donna and you're the only who can help me. Did she say where she was going?"

"No."

"Maybe you got some ideas, then. Did she ever talk about what places she liked? Probably some fishing town or other, someplace for that bastard Fletcher."

"I honestly don't know. Donna took pains not to say where she was going."

Judy reached abruptly for another cigarette. "And from the sound of it, you don't care, neither. Doesn't matter to you, I guess, if a baby never sees her momma."

"No, you don't understand." I opened the icebox and brought out a couple of beers. The gesture seemed to soothe her.

"I'm sorry," she said. "Here I am, getting on you, and you ain't done nothing wrong."

"Don't be so sure."

She seemed puzzled by that, but she went on. "I mean, I ain't proud of some of the things I've done. But I think if I just get another chance, I can do right by her—" Her eyes filled suddenly, and her voice broke as she said, "I know it's hard for you to believe this, but I miss my baby *so much*."

I handed her a bar napkin, and her hands shook as she dried her cheeks.

"Do you know how hard it is to live with yourself... knowing that you turned your back..." She inhaled suddenly and seemed to find a new resolve. "But that's all in the past now. Sharlene deserves better than what she's gotten, and starting now I'm going to make up for everything I ever did to let her down."

I knew what I had to say—but not how to say it. All I could think about was a tiny earring sinking slowly into the green.

"Tell me something," I said hoarsely. "Was it you or Donna who had Sharlene's ears pierced?"

Judy seemed relieved.

"That was me," she said. "Two little cultured pearls. Sharlene put up a hell of a squawk when I pierced 'em, but them pearls really set her apart, don't they?"

I could put it off no longer.

"Judy, I'm sorry. I'm very, very sorry—"

A flash of anger crossed her face. She thought I was refusing to help.

"Sharlene is dead."

"What?" Her eyes moved frantically about the room, and she pulled her purse to her lap. "What do you mean, Sharlene's—"

"She drowned, Judy. I think she must have fallen off Fletcher's boat the last night they were here. Donna and Fletcher are gone, but they found Sharlene yesterday."

Her face stiffened. "Bunny...Bunny didn't say nothing about...how do you know this?"

"When Donna got your card Saturday night, they all went for a last ride on the boat before they left town. They must have been out around Redfish Island, because, well, they found her there a couple of days later."

Judy clenched her eyes shut, and they began to run again. I moved next to her and reached for her shoulder.

"Don't!" she said. "Just get—please, just leave me alone!"

She slowly gathered herself and looked up again, dreading more details.

"There's no delicate way to put this, Judy. Even though there's no doubt it was Sharlene, it has become difficult to positively identify the body. The police say if they had something to go on, medical records, a birth certificate maybe—"

"Police," she said numbly, and as the word sank in her

expression grew hard. "I don't think...no, I better not."

"But they need to—"

"I don't care," she said, suddenly defiant. "I can't afford to...get in trouble...get mixed up in this."

My surprise seemed to make her more certain.

"Cops...I don't want nothing to do with no cops. I'll probably wind up in jail myself for letting her go."

"I thought you'd want to help."

"Well, you thought wrong." Her voice began to quaver. "Sounds like...sounds like I can't help her no more anyway...poor thing..."

She tried to use her cigarette, but her hand wasn't steady enough. She threw it to the floor and spilled her beer when she stood.

"I've got to go," she blurted. "Thank you for your...I, I've really got to go."

I followed her to the parking lot, insisting there were ways she might help the police with Sharlene—and maybe even with Donna. When Judy started to close her car door, I grabbed it with both hands.

"Don't you have a conscience?" I shouted. "Don't you feel any responsibility at all?"

"Don't you preach to me. I was fucked up—I, I made a mistake—but I've tried to get her back ever since, by God. Didn't I fucking try?"

She saw my grip weaken.

"But you didn't try, did you? If you'd turned Donna in like you should have, Sharlene would—"

I dropped my hands and watched her roar away, crying convulsively as she headed for wherever it was she'd planned to take her baby. When finally I turned back to my room, Bunny was on the steps outside her office, smiling contemptuously.

"She's right, you know. That little bitch had you nailed, Sam."

I stood flat-footed on the oyster shell, unable to answer.

"If you'd only done the right thing—"

"But...but she belonged with Donna," I said. "Donna was better for her than this...this Judy."

"Maybe, maybe not. We'll never know, now will we? But I know one thing, buddy boy. If you'd turned in Donna—and you know you should have—that baby would still be alive."

"You," I said weakly. "You knew about Sharlene all along."

"Yes, I did."

"And still you blame me."

"Yes, I do."

I looked down at my palms, hardened now by a summer of this life, and imagined what it would be like to hold pieces of her translucent skin in them. Sharlene, I wondered, who is it that *you* blame?

When no answer came, I glanced at the bay and wished I had never seen it. For the rest of my life it would remind me of the silence of her hands.

"You was that baby's only hope, Sam. I knew what Fletcher was capable of, and I knew he'd have killed me if I told."

"You're lying," I said. "That old fool was too broken to hurt a fly."

"Now you're the one lying, Sam. I heard about the show-down he had with that Mexican during the street dance. They tell me you was sitting right next to him when it happened. So you know as well as I do what that man's capable of.

"He was crazy about that baby, Sam, stark raving crazy. Even if I'd turned them in with a phone call, anonymous, it wouldn't have made no difference. Him and Donna knew none of these low-lifes was ever gonna squeal, so he'd have come right on and killed me."

Bunny glared at the sky.

"But when you got tight with Donna, I knew it was safe to tell you. She wouldn't have let him touch you—or she'd have warned you to hit the road. So I let you in on the secret, Sam, thinking a nice educated boy would do the right thing."

Bunny paused to savor my agony. Out on the creek the

bridge horn sounded, and I pictured a sailboat making the unholy passage from the outside world to the bay.

"So," I heard myself rasp. "You had it all figured out."

She sneered down at me and shook her head.

"No I didn't, Sam. Turns out Donna had you pegged better than I did."

*　*　*

The police later told me the trail to Judy Cason went cold in a trailer park west of Victoria, where she had skipped out owing two months rent the year before. No birth records could be found for a two-year-old girl named Cason. Judy had apparently delivered her with out the benefit—or the documentation—of a doctor.

Donna Bedicek and Fletcher Quinn proved just as elusive. I knew Donna had a sister, but I didn't know where she lived, or even if she still used her maiden name. There was no trace of a fatherless Quinn family in Biloxi. They might have taken on a stepfather's name or started fresh in another town. And it was just as easy to believe Fletcher had fabricated his entire past.

The case soon began to fade away. And in the end, the only evidence that Sharlene Cason had ever lived was in a manila folder in a green file cabinet in the back of a stuffy storage room.

In the days and weeks that followed, my love for the waterfront began slowly to wither and fail. Sunrises and sunsets became featureless events in the dog days of August. Beer joints held the same faces, docks the same boats and creaky piles. Even the long trips back from the bay lost their majesty. I felt a kind of shame for myself and everyone on the creek.

After a summer of stirring involvements, I was suddenly alone again. Even Knuckles lost his new boat and spent most of the season in Rockport. But the greatest loss of all was Donna. I wanted nothing so much as to see her again, to talk to her, to have her explain why everything had suddenly gone so wrong.

There was never a word from her, of course. It would have been foolish to contact me after what happened, and I never should have expected it. But every trip to the post office was lightened with a hope that I'd find a letter from Donna.

I told myself again and again that she had been a noble woman, after all. In spite of her flaws, and despite what I knew in my soul to be only a terrible accident, I concluded that Sharlene died in the custody of her rightful mother. I wanted to believe—and have tried to believe ever since—that leaving her with Donna was the right thing to do.

But that belief brought little solace. And it did nothing to alter the central, terrible fact: Leaving Sharlene with Donna preserved a sequence of events that sent a two-year-old girl to her grave.

*   *   *

Roy and I had a bountiful season, but as the shrimping petered out in autumn, I knew it was time for me to go. The lingering tragedy of August had shaken the glamour out of the life by then, and the harsh rigors of oystering in winter held no appeal at all. Everyone braced for a hurricane that blew up suddenly in October, and I felt a quiet sadness when it spent itself offshore.

I wound up, by default, in Fort Worth, and sank heavily into the soft seat of my father's body shop. It didn't stir my soul to drive to work every morning, but neither did it hurt. Donna and the waterfront had convinced me to taper my aspirations—survival now seemed to be all that I could handle.

My father finally opted out of the working world and settled in a cabin on Eagle Mountain Lake. Dad spent his last years happily enough, catching fish and congratulating me for my sound and sensible commitments.

I never burdened him with my reasons for leaving the bay. He formed theories of his own, theories that made his own life a little easier to take. Meanwhile, I moved efficiently from day to night to day, doing everything I could to wipe every bit of trouble from my mind.

Eighteen

And then one night, working late and alone in my office, I saw her.

Donna had taken the chance, walked up to the lighted window and tapped softly upon it. At first I saw nothing but her gray eyes—and was carried back at once to a warm morning in the marina eight years before. She peered in with her unforgettable wariness. Then she winked, something I had never seen from those eyes before, and swung open the door.

I sank back into my chair when she entered, wearing tight western clothes and layered, shoulder-length hair. She smiled broadly, displaying rows of perfect white teeth that for some reason made me uncomfortable.

Her smile evaporated when she saw the effect it had on me. Immediately her face began to reflect every stunted emotion I'd felt since she ran to Fletcher's boat in Adelia. Yes, it was Donna. And she could still penetrate me with the quickest glance.

"Well," she finally said, "how's about a hug for your long-lost friend?"

My arms found the same firm flesh on her back. She held the embrace even when I started to move away, and I felt myself begin to cling tighter.

"You look so good, Sam. You did the smart thing leaving the water. It ages people too fast."

She took a chair, threw one leg over the other, and gave a

guilty grin as she pulled a pack of cigarettes from her purse.

"Look at this," she said. "Death wish, I guess."

Donna was wearing faded jeans and a frilly blouse that rasped audibly against her brassiere. I sat on my desk and asked how she had found me.

"Just let my fingers do the walking, Sam. I figured you might wind up in your daddy's business before it was over with. Been getting up the nerve to do this for months."

For *months*. Hardly a day had passed without my thinking of Donna, and she'd been stalking me for months.

"So," I said, a little too eagerly, "you live in Fort Worth?"

She shrugged. "Let's not get into that. Just tell me everything about you."

"Not much to say, really. I finally decided I was kidding myself on the water—I wasn't cut out for that. And this...this seemed as safe a harbor as any."

Donna took a long, nervous drag on her cigarette.

"Tell me," I said, "how's Fletcher?"

"Dead."

"God, I—I'm sorry."

"Don't be. He ran off pretty soon after we left the creek. They told me he had a stroke or something in his sleep, and it put him straight out of his misery."

Donna grinned bitterly and reached for an ashtray. I began to feel squeamish. *It put him straight out of his misery.* Was that what brought her here—a desire to end her own misery?

Or was it simpler than that? It was just as possible she was acting on the kind of guilty impulse that had brought Judy Cason to my apartment. If it was cleansing forgiveness Donna wanted, I was the last person in the world who could give it.

"You haven't mentioned—" I said suddenly. "—how is Sharlene getting along?"

She glared at me for a second, then looked away.

"Don't ask me, Sam. Her mother took her back years ago."

"She found you, did she?"

"That's right—hey, I said we weren't going to talk about me."

The magic was already failing, and we both knew it. I remembered the bottle of Canadian in my desk. Donna laughed edgily when she saw it. I poured a couple of drinks, and she drained hers without tasting it.

"Ever go back to the marina, Sam?"

"No. Guess I'm not up to it. How about you?"

"Haven't seen it since the night we left the boat there. It's probably been blown away three or four times since then."

Donna pulled out another cigarette. She wanted to tell me the truth, but she was losing her nerve.

"Donna, why did you look me up after all this time?"

She sighed and held out her glass for a refill.

"You and me...we were something, weren't we, Sam?"

"Yeah, the perfect mismatch."

"That summer we had, it was the happiest time of my life. Better than when me and Fletcher had it good, even."

She let some whiskey pool on her tongue before she swallowed.

"How about you, Sam? You feel the same way?"

"Yes."

"Sometimes, maybe once in your life if you're lucky, everything seems to come together, you know? Just for a minute, maybe, but there it is."

I asked Donna to tell me about her minute.

"Believe it or not, it was the night of the street dance—right after Bunny gave me that card. I just decided that whatever it took, I was gonna keep Sharlene. That was—"

She dropped her glass to the carpet and sobbed into her fists. "Oh, Sam, how come we have to keep living?"

I knelt beside her and touched the soft hair at her temple. Part of me wanted to pull it back into a golden ponytail and watch it bounce between her shoulders. She looked out through her tears and despaired again of telling me.

"Donna, I know Sharlene is dead."

Her eyes expanded in horrified grief.

"They found her out by Redfish a couple of days after the dance."

She turned away and rocked at the waist like an autistic child.

"Fletcher got so drunk," she cried. "Cussing, screaming, swinging at me and Sharlene if we ever got close to him. He made us stay back on the deck, said women didn't belong in the wheelhouse.

"Pretty soon we're coming up on the channel, and there's a big tanker in it, riding high on the water. Fletcher's headed straight for it full blast, like he wants to kill us all. I ran inside and he was laughing, crazy laughing, saying how does it feel to have my life in his hands for a change. I fought him for the wheel and he veered off at the last minute—missed the damn ship by a couple of feet. I ran out back and Sharlene was gone."

Donna clenched her eyes and shivered at the memory.

"There wasn't no finding her out in the dark like that. We went all up and down the channel for hours, even though we knew there wasn't no hope. And the thing of it was, Fletcher said he wasn't going to hit the ship—he just wanted to throw a scare into me. If I hadn't wrestled with him, if I'd only trusted him…"

She swallowed back the taste of eight ruined years and looked down at me—and for the briefest instant it seemed as though no time had passed. We were still in the marina and I was still listening, still transfixed by the woman I loved.

But just as suddenly the spell was broken, when she reached down for her glass and tilted it for another refill.

"Tell me the truth, Sam. That terrible thing, that's how come you left the water, wasn't it? Me…it was me that ruined your plans."

"Plans. You were the one with the plans, remember?"

Donna choked on a laugh.

"Yeah, I had some big plans for a couple of seconds, didn't I? Funny, everything would have been different that night if I'd listened to you."

I began to feel an invisible, oppressive weight. Donna watched me slump back to an elbow, and she pushed her chair away to sit on the floor beside me.

"Remember them days in Tina's?" she said. "All them long talks we used to have?"

I closed my eyes and nodded.

"And remember that night at Grady's? You know, that night I told you all about Sharlene?"

"That was the night that killed her," I heard myself say. "If I had done something about it then, Sharlene would be asleep right now in some warm, safe bed."

Donna looked at me with a growing recognition, and her eyes began to fill again.

"So," she whispered. "Looks like it was you that ruined me, and me that ruined you."

I rolled onto my back and stared at the ceiling. I still loved Donna, and I knew I always would. But I was helpless...incapable of reaching out to draw her near. After a few silent minutes, Donna rose and walked slowly to the door.

She turned back for one last hopeful instant. I had dreamed for eight lonely years of a chance to see Donna again, but I let her open the door and leave me without even watching her go.

Nineteen

I have never been back to the waterfront, but there are nights when my father's cabin takes me there.

Not long after I saw Donna, I wandered out to his fishing dock and found the moon glimmering gently on the lake. The old sights and sounds came back in a rush: pink neon, blinking channel markers, the sudden blare of a jukebox through an open door. My throat even went dry with the creek's insistent stink.

And suddenly I was sitting on the dock at Cutter's again, young and fervently alive, the night Roy anointed me a shrimper. The Silver Dollar was swaying before me, and I remembered how powerful and elegant I felt the first time I stepped aboard.

That night, that crystalline moment, had seemed my life's culmination. It was the night I prevailed over despair, the night of my grand new beginning. But it was also the night I found out about Sharlene, the night Bunny said she was stolen.

A lifetime of dread and doubt...and then at last a chance to reach for the sky. All that stood in the way was an impish little girl and the stern judgment of the bay that it was not for me to act. She belonged, of course, with Donna. But I had no way of knowing it then. I had made the right choice for the most selfish of reasons, and the right choice led to her death.

After a while the smells slowly faded, and the distant

channel lights went black. I found myself staring again into a cool, North Texas sky. For the briefest instant, past and present had come tumbling together, each exposing the other in its ugliest relief. And I knew that all the others who had failed Sharlene were different in a crucial way from me. Donna, Fletcher, Judy, even Bunny, had acted in some way for the girl. In accidental death, guilt attaches to motive. It was I who had blood on his hands.

And so my search ended where it began, on the water, the same place it ended for an old friend of mine. I came to share his conviction that failure can bring with it a tragic yet satisfying peace...

...because on that night, when I thought of Donna, and of Sharlene as last I saw her, I felt my hand slipping, my ankles kicking...until finally, cast loose in the darkness, I was free.

* * *

It was hardly a surprise I could find no Donna Bedicek listed anywhere near Fort Worth. Even if that was still the name she used, there was no reason to believe she'd suddenly invested in a telephone.

My next thought was of the sign outside the body shop, which Dad had built with a marquee large enough to display his pearls of wisdom. I'd never felt sure enough of any idea to commit it to public view, but if Donna had spent months driving secretly past my office, there was a chance she was still out there...

So I rushed back to town from Dad's fishing dock and, by the luster of a buzzing floodlight, reached out to the woman I loved. Over the next weeks no one was indiscreet enough to ask what it was all about, but I'm sure the coffee shops thrummed with speculation. Something had obviously gotten into that Traynor boy, putting a personal message like that in front of his business. Who was this "Donna" person, anyhow? And what does he mean, "Let's wipe every bit of trouble from our minds."?

There were no calls from Donna, no taps at the window. Each passing day brought a rising fear that I'd lost her, this time forever. She'd walked out of my life again without leaving a clue about how to find her—

—or had she?

Sam, how come we have to keep on living?

He had a stroke or something in his sleep, and it put him straight out of his misery.

Donna's mother didn't have to live long after she discovered life didn't keep its promises. Donna had outlived her own broken dreams by eight years—and hinted broadly that it was no longer worth the fight. Perhaps that was why she had wandered back to Fort Worth, the town that ended her mother's anguish, the town that had taught a ten-year-old Donna the price of foolish hope.

Certainly the trappings were there—western clothes, cigarettes, a pair of spiked heels. If I was right, my best chance to find Donna was on Jacksboro Highway, somewhere among the loud and rowdy beer joints that had taken her mother's life.

Had she contacted me in a last, desperate attempt to save herself? Worse, would my numb response move her to seek the same penance that brought her mother peace?

I spent days and nights wandering from bar to bar, trying to describe her, asking if anyone knew her, telling countless bored strangers far more than was necessary about our lives together.

And then, late one night in a bar called The Panther, I was half a beer into my story when the bartender's eyes began to widen.

"Hey, Bill," he shouted to someone in a darkened corner. "Come take a listen at this."

A large, graying, wax-faced man on crutches lumbered up to the bar. His left leg was bandaged up to his Bermuda shorts, and he had a bagged fifth of something strapped to one of the crutches. He looked at me expectantly.

"He's looking for some gal," the bartender said. "I got an idea you might be able to help. Go ahead, mister. Tell him what you told me."

"Well, she's about forty now, and she wears dentures. But she looks fantastic, with these cool gray eyes and an incredible body. We used to work together on Galveston Bay about eight years ago—and out of the blue she came to see me recently.

"Like an idiot, I let her get away. But I've just got to see her again. She had light brown hair in a pony tail in the old days, but this last time it was fixed up in waves and layers."

Bill gave the bartender a knowing look.

"Go ahead, mister, tell Bill what her name is."

"Donna," I said eagerly. "Donna Bedicek."

The bartender stepped away from us. Bill shifted his crutches so he could face me directly.

"So," he said sadly. "She seen you here recently?"

"Yes, yes. Do you know her?"

"Matter of fact, I do. And the truth of it is, I feel like I know you, too. It's Sam Traynor, isn't it, the fella with the body shop?"

I reached deliriously for his hand. "Yes, yes. And who are you, sir?"

He sighed and looked out into the darkened room. "Bill Joyce," he said. "I've been wondering when this day was gonna come."

I grew queasy as it finally began to sink in.

"And you," I mumbled, "You and Donna are—"

"Married, Mr. Traynor. Me and Donna is married."

I slumped back to the stool and reached in a daze for my beer. Bill struggled onto the next seat and hoisted his crutch.

"Can I offer you a drink, Mr. Traynor? I imagine you and me are both about due for a stiff one."

The bartender dropped two glasses of ice in front of us before I could answer.

"I had a feeling Donna was gonna look you up one of these days. She was always afraid to, on account of what happened to that poor little girl and all. But I told her, I said, `Donna, honey, your mind ain't gonna get no rest until you face up to it.'"

He poured a couple of inches into each glass and then raised his for a toast.

"Here's to Sam Traynor," he said calmly, "the only man Donna ever loved."

I was too astonished to reach for my drink. Bill finished his in one swallow and wiped his lips with a thumb.

"She ain't never out-and-out said it, Mr. Traynor, but I know it's true. When a man's been married to a woman for five years, he just knows a thing like that without her even having to tell him."

"I'm...well...I don't know what to say."

"Don't worry, Mr. Traynor. I don't harbor no ill will to no man. I'm gonna be sixty years old this year, and I ain't got enough time left to be using it up on bitterness. Donna—I'm sure you know this—she's a wonderful woman, and what I want most is for her to be happy."

He uncapped the bottle and floated his ice cubes again.

"I expect you're pretty confused, and I don't blame you one bit. I'll tell you where you can find her, but first I'm gonna ask you to hear me out for just a minute. Can you bear with me for that long?"

"Of course."

"Thank you. Well, Donna and me got married real quick after we met. I drive a truck, Mr. Traynor, and she was working at this diner in Waxahachie. My job keeps me on the road most of the time, and it wasn't too long before we realized it wasn't going to work out too good. We've stayed in touch and all, but I guess you might say we're husband and wife in name only."

"I'm sorry," I said. And I was. This gentle, unselfish man deserved better.

"I know it's no fault of yours, Mr. Traynor, but I believe in my heart it was you that come between us. The way she used to talk about you and about the times down on the coast...well, there wasn't no mistaking the way she felt. And there wasn't nothing I could do about it. I was up against a man who wasn't even there.

"So I did the only thing I could think of. I begged her over and over again to look you up, you know, to face up to things once and for all and take it wherever it went to. But she wouldn't hear of it—said she knew you'd never forgive her for what happened.

"And then here about six months ago she says she's gonna move to Fort Worth. With my job it don't much matter where I live, so I pretty much made this my home base, too. I could tell things were sort of coming to a head for Donna, and I wanted to be around in case she needed somebody.

"But I've known her long enough to realize I'm only fooling myself. It's you she needs, Mr. Traynor, not me.

"Anyhow, the long and short of it is this. You've got to forgive her, Mr. Traynor. It looks to me like you're the only one in the world who can give Donna another chance."

*   *   *

Donna's trailer was a few blocks from Jacksboro Highway, on the west end near Lake Worth. The door was open, and through the screen I could hear the shower running. I waited outside on the steps and rehearsed what I was going to say.

Donna, you said we ruined each other. If that's true, we're the only ones who can make each other well...

We're just like we were in the beginning, Donna. You're drifting along day by day, and I'm losing myself under a pile of plans. Let's try again to forgive one another, to save one another. I love you too much to let it fail...

It wasn't that I didn't want you when you found me. It wasn't that I didn't love you as much as anyone can love. I let you walk away because I was powerless to stop you. Until now I had nothing of myself to give...

Donna stepped into the hallway in a damp terry bathrobe, with a white towel wrapped over her hair. She hesitated when she saw me, then rushed to the door in tears. We rocked in each other's arms to the sweet, silent music of redemption and knew we had found our way at last.

Words wouldn't come, but neither of us needed them. There was a short road leading to the shore of Lake Worth, where we slipped free of our clothes in the moonlight and let the warm, sandy current rinse our souls.